MW01127877

THE TATTOO ARTIST

BY

CAROL L. GANDOLFO

Cover Photo by Bill Dahl

PROLOGUE

Current Day - Las Vegas, Nevada

SIN CITY. LAS VEGAS. Where you can buy anything or do anything. Millions of tourists come each year to lose money, to marry, to divorce, to get drunk, to gamble their life savings or just to make fools of themselves. I decided to use Las Vegas as my hideout. It's a great place to get lost or just to disappear. Or so I thought.

Warm Spring winds blew as I parked in the Greyhound Terminal lot. There were only a few cars, but tourists filled the bus terminal on South Main. A group of twenty or so young Japanese teens huddled around a tour guide. They wore bright yellow T-shirts with pictures of Mickey or Minnie Mouse. Almost every one of them sported an edgy Anime-style haircut, making it almost impossible to distinguish gender. I took a guess and figured out the girls donned Minnie Mouse and the males wore Mickey. Just past the group of tourists, glum individuals occupied the benches. I wondered how many had lost their mortgage payment and were afraid to go home and face family.

I located locker 499 at the end of a long row along the back wall of the terminal. There were numerous red-tagged keys still in the locks. I inserted mine, opened the locker and took out the last of my money, leaving the key in the slot. I

stuffed the package into the bottom of my
backpack lying on the floor. A loud bang
sounded behind me and I jumped, hitting my
head on the still-open door. I checked for
bullet wounds. None. I was still in one
piece.

When I turned, a young man dropped to
his knees and picked up a broken stapler
and several neon-orange papers. Long brown
wavy hair, streaked with blonde and worn in
a ponytail, hung down from a backward
baseball cap. Tattoos covered his arms. The
tattoo on his right forearm caught my
attention. A beautiful mermaid swam up his
bicep through a deep blue ocean. Fish
cavorted beside her and seaweed wrapped
around her tail. Her upper body looked
muscled, yet sensuous. The scales on the
lower part of her turquoise figure
shimmered as she raced for the surface. The
man turned, as if sensing my gaze. Now that
my heart had stopped thumping in my chest,
I approached him.

"Can I help?" I stepped closer.

He nodded. He had deep-set, gray-blue
eyes. He wore a trimmed mustache and a
shaped beard decorated his round face. I
knelt and handed him papers from the floor.
After we had scooped up all the papers, he
stood, took one flyer and pinned it to the
bulletin board next to him. I looked at the
flyer, which advertised a local tattoo
parlor. I remembered an art gallery in New
York, show casing Shotsie, considered one

of the top tattoo artists in the country. The advertisement gave me an idea.

I slung my backpack over my shoulder. "Hey, is this parlor looking for an apprentice?"

His eyes crinkled, like a young Santa. "Well," he looked straight at me. "It's my parlor and it depends." He reached into his back pocket and pulled out a neatly folded handkerchief and handed it to me. "You're bleeding."

Confused, I took the cloth.

"Your forehead," he said.

"I can pay," I dabbed at my face.

He raised his eyebrows and chuckled. "Well, I might consider an apprentice. Can you draw?"

"I'm the best." I lied.

"Adam," He stuck the flyers under his arm and put out his hand.

"Nikki Flowers." I said.

He enveloped my hand in a large beefy one and shook it vigorously.

"Where's your shop?"

"On Fremont, just east of The Strip. You can't miss it." He handed me one of the papers. "Can you come by tomorrow around three and show me some of your artwork?"

"Sure, see you then." I left him putting his stapler back together. I still held his handkerchief. I turned and called back, "What about your hankie?"

"I've got a drawer full. Don't worry about it." With that, he stapled another flyer on the bulletin board.

DRAWING TATTOOS WASN'T my original plan, but it seemed the only way to do art and stay hidden. In fact, I dreamed of being an artist, to hang paintings in a gallery and maybe someday owning a gallery of my own. Right then, that didn't look like much of a possibility. With what I had done, tattoos would probably be the closest I would ever come to be an artist.

I shoved the flyer into my hip pocket and left the station. There was a lot to do by tomorrow afternoon.

With my keys pressed in my palm, I hurried across the parking lot. My ten-year old red Toyota Corolla sat under a fluorescent light thick with dancing moths. I jumped in and locked the door before throwing the bag onto the seat beside me. The new engine roared to life and I drove away from the bus station.
☐

ONE

Thirteen Years Earlier

AFTER A WEEK AWAY, Daddy was coming home. I tingled with excitement to hear all about the news he promised to share with us. It was probably something about some big buildings. I didn't understand everything, but Dad had told Mom things would change our lives. What was Dad going to tell us when he got home?

Since Mom and I had already cleaned up the living room, I cleaned my room and spent the next hour picking up my toys and putting them away. The walls were light colors with my drawings tacked on the walls. I loved all colors, but not pink. The only pink in my room was a pink horse. I straightened my bed and put my dirty clothes in the hamper. Done with that, I took my favorite book from the shelf. Dad always read part of Cinderella before I went to sleep, and I wanted to be prepared for tonight. The pages had been turned repeatedly, the cover was faded and the pages worn. I gently placed it on the bed.

I went into the closet, leaving the door open a crack. This was my safe place. In the comfort of the dark, I put on my favorite red and white checked dress. I sat on a stool, slipped off my tennis shoes and put on lace anklets and black patent leathers. For several minutes, I sat in the dark, enjoying the quiet. When I came out,

I went to the pale-yellow table my father made for me two years ago. At seven, I would outgrow it soon, but now, I was still able to swing my feet as I pulled out paper and my box of crayons.

The drawing in front of me took over an hour. Every flower had to be just so. I was putting on the finishing touches when my elbow bumped the box. Sixty-four wax sticks rolled across the table and tumbled to the carpet, scattering in *all directions. I dropped down and* searched. Where was my lemon-yellow crayon? One by one, I picked up the crayons and dropped them into a basket. Hiding just under the edge of my bedspread was the bright yellow I searched for. I let out a sigh and went back to my drawing. I used the yellow, then picked up Cornflower Blue and put the final touches on my picture and sat back. I waited.

Several minutes later, I left my room and found my mother sitting in her favorite chair next to the living room window. Afternoon beams of sunlight lit the room. Tiny bits of dust flitted through the rays from the setting sun. Mother's golden hair glowed like Cinderella's as she read her book.

"I brought you a present," I said loudly, interrupting her.

Mom looked up, a serious look on her face. "Mandy, where did you get that butterfly?"

"I made it." The wings of the yellow and blue butterfly slowly moved up and down.

Mother put her book down and stood. "Only God can make butterflies. Did you go outside?"

"No," I insisted. "I made it."

She came closer and looked at the beautiful insect on my finger, its wings stirring. "Did you open your window?"

"No, Mommy. I drew it."

The colorful insect took off and soared around the room.

My mother watched the butterfly and then went to the front door and opened it wide. After circling the foyer, it left the house and flew into a tree.

"My butterfly!" I yelled. "You let him go."

My mother closed the door and turned to face me. "Now I'm going to ask you one more time. Did you go outside?" She placed her hands on her hips and her eyebrows came together.

"I didn't go outside, Mom."

Mom sighed. "You know how your father and I feel about lying."

"I'm not, Mom."

"Okay, I don't want to argue now. I have to get dinner ready. Your Dad should be home soon, so go to your room and wash up. I'll call you down when it's ready."

Mom turned and went into the kitchen. Defeated, I headed up to my bedroom to pout.

I spent the next hour, drawing something safe: flowers. When Mom announced dinner, I went downstairs.

"Dinner's ready," she told me when I reached the bottom of the stairs. "Daddy must be running late. So, you can go ahead and eat."

Mom looked at my dress and smiled. "You look pretty. But let's put on a napkin so you don't get stained."

Just as I sat down to a plate of spaghetti, the doorbell rang.

"Dad must have forgotten his key. Go ahead and start eating." She wiped her hands on her apron and went to the front door.

I heard the door open and a male's voice. I stopped with a fork full of pasta halfway to my mouth when my mother screamed.

THE SPAGHETTI FELL off my fork and I ran into the hall, holding the fork high. The wood floor was slippery. I grabbed onto the wall to keep my footing. When I turned the corner, I saw a man in a gray suit lean down on one knee and reach for my mother.

"Don't you hurt my Mom," I jumped on the man, stabbing him in the hand with the fork. He screamed and fell on his butt. A man in a blue suit and a thick mustache reached for me. I pulled away and kicked at the man now on the ground.

"Officer Foley, please." The man in the blue suit called.

Out of the corner of my eye, I saw a black clad figure move around the two men and my mother was now on the floor. Strong hands pulled me off the man and held me in the air. I kicked out again and connected with the groin of the man in blue. He screamed and doubled over. My mother slumped to the floor.

"Officer Foley! Some help here please." The man in gray wrapped a cloth around his bleeding hand.

The female police officer squeezed me slightly and whispered in a husky voice. "It's okay, honey. No one is hurting your mom."

I turned and glared into her tanned, oval face. Her large chocolate eyes were soft. I stopped fighting when I recognized a police uniform. "Why did she fall?" I asked.

Officer Foley avoided my question. "Just look. She's okay."

Officer Foley turned me toward the two men. The man in gray now held my mother while she sobbed. The handkerchief on his hand was soaked with blood. The man in the blue suit, on the porch, vomited into my mother's flower bed.

Still holding me in her arms, Officer Foley set me on the floor and took my hand. "Let's go to the kitchen and let the adults talk."

In the living room, both men were now sitting with my mother. The man in the blue suit's skin appeared the same gray color as the other man's suit.

"Sorry," I said.

Mom had a wad of tissues in her hand and was sobbing quietly. The man in the gray suit patted her on the shoulder.

"What did he tell my mom?" I insisted.

"I'll let your mother tell you. Is there someone we can call to help your mom?"

"What for?"

"Well, can we call your grandparents?" Office Foley walked me to the kitchen and looked around.

"Grandma and Grandpa are dead." I said defiantly.

"What about your other grandparents?" she asked.

Bored, I climbed up on a stool at the counter and began to swing my feet. "I don't have any other grandparents. Now can I go see my mom?"

"Is there anyone else I can call to come be with your mother?"

I let out a loud sigh. "Why don't you just call my Dad?"

She looked down at the floor. "Honey, we can't call your father right now. Doesn't your mom have a good friend I can call?"

"Well, you could call Uncle Carlo."
"Is he your mom's brother or your father's brother?"

I was getting tired of all the stupid questions. "He's Daddy's business partner." With that, I stood up. "I'm going back to Mom."

"Okay, but can you first help me find Carlo's phone number?"

"Come on." I took her hand and took her to a drawer in the kitchen. She opened it and pulled out a personal phonebook.

"What's Carlo's last name?" She ruffled through the book.

"Rinaldi," I stood tapping my shoe on the floor.

"Amanda," Officer S. Foley, said. "Would you please wait for me upstairs?"

"Sure," I walked out of the kitchen, stopping just outside the door and listening. Officer Foley lowered her voice, but what I heard brought my world to an end and I raced up the stairs and slammed my bedroom door. I grabbed my drawing pad and crayons and began to work furiously. Minutes later, Officer Foley opened the door and peeked inside.

"Amanda, are you okay?"

I ignored her and continued to work on my drawing. When done, I threw my crayons aside, grabbed my drawing, and ran down the stairs. I plopped down on the bottom step and waited.

Officer Foley came and knelt beside me. "I'm so sorry."

I ignored her and waited. When she touched me, I pulled away.

"Wait." I sat on the stairs and watched the front door. She sat down beside me.

"What are we waiting for?"

"You'll see." We sat in silence, listening to the voices of the men in gray and blue suits as they soothed Mom. Finally, the doorbell rang.

"He's here." I got up, ran to the door and yanked it open. Carlo stood at the front door. I peered around him. Daddy's not there. "Where is he?"

"Daddy's not coming home," Mom said as she came into the hallway.

"No!" I screamed. "You're lying."

"Come home, Daddy. Please." I looked down at the drawing in my hand.

Mom came up to me and lifted me up. "He was in a car accident."

I put my head on her shoulder. "I tried, Mom."

"Tried what, Mandy?"

"I tried to bring Daddy home." I said softly. "But it didn't work."

Mom stroked my hair and I let the drawing fall to the floor.

TWO

Current Day

I LEFT THE GREYHOUND terminal and
headed north. I drove straight home,
forsaking my normal circuitous routes.
When I arrived in Vegas two years earlier,
my first task was to place several packages
in a bus locker. It didn't seem smart to
drive around town with two suitcases mostly
filled with cash. After storing the money,
I found a cheap motel just east of the
Strip, unpacked my meager belongings and
took care of my next plan.

At a junkyard, I watched as the car I
bought in New York was crushed into a
block. Afterward, I hired a taxi and went
to a used car lot where I purchased my
little red Toyota from an eager salesman.
He shook my hand and assured me it was a
great deal, but I knew I had spent too much
money. Finally, I searched for the perfect
apartment.

As luck would have it, several
apartments were available for immediate
move in. I chose one at the edge of a
neighborhood where working class singles
lived adjacent to welfare mothers on
Section 8 housing. I signed the lease for
the two-bedroom apartment, adding a
roommate to my lease. Then I visited
several used furniture stores and purchased
a slightly worn bedroom and living room
set. After I bought the essential linens

and kitchen supplies at the local Walmart, I vacated the motel and moved into my new digs.

Now, almost two years later, the two-story building loomed in the darkness. The faded peach paint appeared gray in the moonlight. I drove to the alley behind the building and pulled my car into a stall in the carport. The evening light created shadows in every corner of the complex. Only after parking did it occur to me I had done so without making sure I wasn't followed. I waited. Though no other cars pulled into the alley or lights passed on the street, I shivered. Just to calm my nerves, I got out of the car and went through the building next door. I scanned the street. Seeing nothing, I returned to the alley and entered my own building through the rear.

The building appeared old and uncared for. Patches of peeling paint clung to rusty railings. I walked up the five concrete steps to an empty courtyard. A few old chairs occupied the open area and two large pots with wilted palms sat on each side of the main entrance. I dashed through the empty courtyard and entered my home. Over the last two years, I tried to make my apartment livable by slowly replacing the used furniture with economical but nice furniture and painting the walls soft beige. I accented the apartment with plants, pillows and other objects from Pier

One. Nice, but not ostentatious. Several of my drawings decorated the walls.

Upon entering the apartment, I closed the drapes and went into the second bedroom. I dropped the backpack on the bed and took out the package. Then I ripped open the brown paper bag and dumped out stacks of hundred dollar bills. I looked at the pile of money for a moment then headed to the bathroom to change.

I stood in front of the mirror and stared at my reflection. My eyes were red from the thick eyeliner that blackened my upper and lower lids. Dark burgundy lipstick covered my lips, giving my pale skin a ghostly cast. I pulled off the black spiked wig and threw it on the counter next to several bottles of expensive perfume. I removed eight faux pierced earrings from my earlobes and one from my left nostril and I took in a deep breath. I wrapped a thick towel around my long auburn hair. I applied cleansing cream to my face and wiped off most of the makeup. Finally, I looked more human.

I took off my all-black outfit and slipped into a robe. From the pantry, I took ten Zip-lock sandwich bags, went back to the second bedroom and sat on the bed. I then separated the money. When there were ten bags of $5,000 each, I took off the cover of the heating vent and carefully placed them in next to several bundles already inside the small space. Tomorrow, most of the money would go into one of the many safety deposit boxes around town that held my cash. Spread throughout the different banks, I had over two million dollars just in Vegas. Tonight, however, I had other things to do.

Hot water cascaded over my tired body as I stood in the shower. I scrubbed the rest of the makeup from my face and washed my hair, while enjoying aromas of vanilla and lavender. Feeling refreshed, I stepped out of the shower and rewrapped my long hair in a soft towel and slipped back into the robe.

With a light salad and hot mug of Good Earth tea, I sat in front of my laptop and Googled tattoo art. I knew very little about tattoos and wouldn't think of tattooing myself, but I needed to know more about the process before I met with Adam the next day. It seemed easy enough. Mostly drawing. I found expertvillage.com and watched video after video on the process. This should be easy. I also Googled "Shotsie," not remembering the tattoo artist's last name and found Shotsie Gorman's website. His tattoos were mesmerizing. When I could no longer keep my eyes open, I shut down the computer and climbed under the covers. That night I dreamed of unique designs, but this time they were on bodies rather than on canvas.

THE SOUND OF SOFT jazz drifted into the room as the clock radio announced morning.

I jumped out of bed and pulled the top part of the drapes open, leaving the bottom part closed with a clip. Then I jumped back into bed. Prisms of light danced around the ceiling, reflected off small crystals hanging in the bedroom window. I was just getting warm when

I remembered my task for today and quickly got out of bed and reached for my drawing pad. I turned to a clean page and drew angels, demons, flowers and every design I had found on the Internet as samples of tattoos. Of course, I added my own unique style.

At one-thirty, I put down my pencil. My stomach growled and startled me. I needed food. I threw together a turkey sandwich. I nibbled while I repeated the process of putting on excessive makeup and fake piercings. Then I donned the spiked wig from yesterday. The outfit for today consisted of black leggings, a short faux-leather skirt and a black t-shirt covered with a white lace top. I needed something light to ward off the desert heat. I finished off the entire outfit with a pair of clunky, ankle-high boots. Too late to go to the bank today, I rushed out the door. The money remained safe for one more night.

LAS VEGAS TATTOO, near the corners of Fremont and Las Vegas Boulevards, was a short distance from the old strip. I parked east of the parlor and walked past several homeless individuals and an old woman pushing an overladen shopping cart down the middle of Fremont. A bell above the door clanged with a metallic sound as I entered. I stood for a few seconds, surprised. Instead of the dark cramped space I'd imagined, Las Vegas Tattoo looked much like a hair salon. Samples of tattoos, neatly placed, covered the entire right side of the parlor. Tasteful chairs and small sofas adorned the reception area with a case serving as the reception counter. Down the left side of the large room were four cubicles with half-walls separating them from the large room. I heard a faint humming from one of the cubicles. The display case in front showed numerous belly-button charms, toe rings and some odd glass objects, which I suspected were bongs.

A woman, only slightly older than I, sat behind the waist-high glass counter picking at her cuticles and chomping on gum. She had pink-tipped, blonde spiked hair and a tee-shirt shredded at the shoulders. Between chomps, she would stop picking her fingernails and tap keys on the laptop in front of her, which she studied intently. I walked up to the counter and spoke.

"Hi, I'm here to see Adam."

The pink hair lifted to expose large deep blue eyes. She looked like a young Meg Ryan before all the surgery. She nodded, closed her computer and stood. I stepped back. She was at least four or five inches taller than my five foot six. I looked down expecting to see five-inch heels, but instead saw flat sandals. She turned from me and walked toward the back of the shop. Her skirt was short and showed long, shapely legs. I was convinced she could only be a showgirl at night. She entered a hallway through some hanging beads and knocked on a door. A few seconds later, she seemed to glide back to the front of the salon.

"He'll be out in a minute." She sat back down on the stool, wrapped her long legs around the legs of the stool and went back to her computer. Without looking up, she said, "Go ahead and have a seat."

At the back of the room, a door opened and Adam walked through the beads and came toward us. He wore a long black t-shirt, decorated with a smiling skull; calf-length black, baggy shorts and bulky tennis shoes.

"Hi," he said. "How do you like it?" He waved his hand, indicating the large room. The blonde kept smacking away on her gum.

"It's great," I handed him his handkerchief, clean and neatly folded. From my backpack I pulled out my sketchbook, opened it to the drawings I had drawn that morning and handed the pad to him. He took it and sat down in a plastic chair in the sitting area. He began flipping through the drawings. I waited without a word,

listening to the steady smack of the
blonde's gum. Adam nodded a few times as he
flipped through my drawings. When he came
to the end of the pad, I started to reach
for it. He pulled back, flipped to the
beginning and looked at my first drawings.
    "Oh, don't bother with those," I
started. He ignored me and turned one page
after another until he came to the page I
had originally shown him.

    "Wow," he said as he handed back the
book. "You've really got talent. Have you
had any formal training?"

    I hesitated for just a moment. "Well,
uh, no. Just a few high school art
classes."

    "Have you ever done a tat?"

    "No."

    The smacking had stopped and the blonde
now looked up. He glanced at her, stood and
touched my arm.

    "Let's go in the back and talk."
The blonde's eyes narrowed as he led me
toward the back room, past the four
cubicles. In one cubicle I could see a man
bent over. Again, I noticed the
intermittent buzzing from the cubicle. When
I stopped, Adam put his fingers to his lips
and motioned me past. Through the back door
there were three more rooms. "Toilet" was
painted on one door toward the back and the

other was closed. The first door stood open and he gestured me to enter a room about ten by ten. More photos of tattoo artwork covered the walls. The middle of the room appeared much like a medical office with a bed, what looked like a dentist's chair and a high table covered with tattooing implements.

"Have a seat," Adam offered as he jumped into the dentist's chair and motioned for me to sit on a stool. Then he showed those white teeth and laughed. "Can I see your tattoos?" he asked. I hesitated for several seconds and when I opened my mouth, he interrupted.

"You don't even have a tattoo, do you?"

My cheeks turned red. "No." The foolish child caught with my hand in the proverbial cookie jar. My cover was blown. And so quickly.

"Hey, that's cool." He reached out and put his hand on my shoulder. "I don't mind teaching you, if you can handle working with me. But you'll have to get tattooed first. You can't tattoo unless you've experienced one yourself. It's an unwritten rule."

"You mean, you'll really teach me?" I asked.

"Sure. Your work reminds me of Shotsie's. Haven't seen anything else like it till now."

"Shotsie? You mean Shotsie Gorman?"

"Yeah," he answered. "I got to work with him once in New York. He's best known for his portraits of Charles Lindbergh and a fireman holding a baby. They're awesome."

"Shotsie was one of my inspirations," I said, hoping he would not ask more about New York. "There was a small gallery in New York showing his work. Wow, what colors."

"You were in New York?"

I caught myself. "Well, yes. Once. On vacation."

As we walked back toward the front of the shop, we again passed the occupied cubicle. The buzzing stopped just as we started to walk by. I peered in. A man held a tattoo needle in his left hand, poised over his right arm. He looked up and put down the needle.

"This is Pete," Adam offered.

Pete picked up some gauze and dabbed at the freshly applied tattoo. He stood and came toward us, his hand extended. He stood about three inches taller than Adam, but all muscle. He wore his hair cut short, and he had two large diamond studs in his ears.

On his head was a red baseball cap with the bill toward the back of his head. Like Adam, he had on a long T-shirt and calf-length shorts.

"Hi," Pete said. I shook his hand, while I stared at his left arm. He gave me a welcoming smile, similar to Adam's. I liked these two men.

"You tattoo yourself?" I said, barely able to contain my surprise.

"Sure," he said. Then he held out his arm for me to see. Except for the last tattoo of a small boy's face, the skin slightly raised and red, the tattoos were actually quite good.

"This is my wife," Pete said pointing to the drawing of a beautiful young woman. "This is my son right after he was born," he pointed to a large-eyed baby.

"And the last one?" I asked.

"That's my son again. He just had his second birthday."

At the front of the parlor Adam turned toward the blonde.

"Pam this is Nikki Flowers. She'll be an apprentice."

"Hello," Pamela said, without offering her hand or a smile. Her eyelids lowered slightly over those intense blue eyes.

Unsure what that meant, I gave her a friendly smile anyway.

"Hi, Pam. I look forward to working with you." Pam just stared without smiling and then went back to her computer.

"You can start by coming in on Monday and Wednesday afternoons around 3:00 p.m. Once you start doing tattoos, you'll get 40 percent of the sale." Adam explained.

"Sure," I said. "What do I pay you for training me?"

"Let's see how you do first." He chuckled.

"Fine. That schedule will work out with my night shift at a local casino," I lied. Thank God he never asked for more details.

"Wait!" Adam called when I turned toward the door. He returned to his workroom and came back with a book in his hand. "You can read this. It will give you a feeling for the history and process of tattooing. That is, if you're serious." I took the large paperback book on the history of tattoos from his outstretched hand. "Yes. I am. Thanks."

That's how I became a tattoo artist. Adam spent a couple of hours letting me watch a few simple tattoos, as long as the customers didn't mind, and in between customers he showed me how to tattoo a

peach, a pear and an orange. I'm going to
be a fruit tattooist. Wait! I'm getting
ahead of myself.
☐

THREE

Thirteen Years Earlier

THE POLICE WERE GONE and Mom tucked me into bed. Then she went back downstairs. The house was quiet. I slid my feet into my slippers and snuck down the stairs. On tiptoes, I walked through the kitchen and hid. My knees pressed against my chest. I watched through the crack between the dining room door and the wall. Carlo sat across from my mother, holding her hands between his large ones.

"I just don't know what to do." My mother's voice cracked. "We both lost our parents, so I have no one to help me with all this."

"I'm here for you."

"Maybe you can help me with getting money for the company. Can you help me with that?" Mom looked up at Carlo.

"Didn't Michael tell you?"

"Tell me what?" Mom tilted her head to the side.

"The company is now mine."

"What? I don't understand. Michael started that company."

"Kathryne, when I came into the company, I made a large investment. It was almost broke. We had an agreement and when Michael died, the entire company reverted to me."

Mom began to cry. "But wasn't there any insurance? Something to take care of Amanda and me?"

"The policy was on his desk, waiting for him to sign it." Carlo explained.

He got up from the chair across from Mom and moved to the couch to sit next to her. He put his arm around her shoulder. "I'm here for you. I can cover your rent. I won't abandon you."

Mom looked over at Carlo and sniffled. "I can't let you take care of me. I'll get a job."

"No," Carlo insisted. "You have a daughter to take care of."

From my hiding place, I watched as Carlo reached for a tissue and dried my mother's eyes. Carlo was taller than my father and darker. According to my father, Carlo was Sicilian, from Southern Italy. Daddy was from Northern Italy and had lighter hair and eyes. I took after my grandmother on my father's side. She was Irish, with my red hair and green eyes. Mom had golden hair and blue eyes.

"There, there," Carlo pulled my mother into his arms and rested his head on her forehead. My mother sobbed and allowed Carlo to hold her. His lips widened in a smile.

After a while, my mother pulled away from Carlo. "Thank you for helping us out. I promise I will pay you back once I get settled."

They continued to talk in quiet voices. My eyelids felt heavy. I couldn't let them find me here, so I got up and quietly made my way from the kitchen. At the foot of the stairs, I found my drawing of Dad. I picked it up and carried it with me to my room. In my room, I found a small velvet pouch, folded the drawing and tucked it inside. I dropped to my knees next to the bed and clutched the bag between my hands.

"God, please keep my daddy safe. I know he is with you now." Back in bed, I fell into a deep sleep.

THE MONTHS FOLLOWING the death of my father were a blur. There was a funeral. People milled about patting me on the top of the head and making strange cooing noises. In my pocket, I always carried the small cloth pouch with the drawing of my father. I carried it everywhere.

Through it all, Carlo Rinaldi was at my mother's side. He became a constant in our lives. He took care of bills, made sure the repairs were made and bought us gifts. After a while, I began to like this tall man. He took good care of mom and me. Even so, I never stopped thinking about Dad.

FOUR

Current Day

THE NEXT MORNING was bank day. Not comfortable with so much money in my hiding place, I needed to visit the bank boxes before the weekend. I made up my mind to go to the Bank of America on the east side of town first.

After my shower, I pulled out a shoulder-length blonde wig and slipped it on. With the wig arranged snugly, I tilted back my head and popped in blue contacts. Once they settled, I looked in the mirror. Being a natural redhead was wonderful, but I needed to change my appearance. My mother's makeup artist, Pietro, had taught me how to do my makeup to change my looks. First, I applied a slightly darker shade of liquid makeup along the sides of my nose to make it appear thinner. A dab at the tip of the nose gave it a shorter appearance. A light brown shadow made my eyes appear deeper set. My mouth was not as wide as Robert's, but my lips were full. A darker lip pencil at the edges caused my mouth to appear wider. Light gloss thinned my lips out. Done.

I studied myself in the mirror. The Jones of New York skirt and blouse were

nice, but not too high end. The current
years over priced fashions made me feel
uncomfortable, so I avoided them. After
shrugging into a lightweight blazer, I
retrieved a leather purse from a secret
storage area in the bottom of the closet in
the second bedroom. What appeared to be a
shelf for shoes was a large wooden box with
a spring hinge. By pressing on the top of
the shoe rack, the hinge popped up and
revealed a large storage space. I took out
a purse and wallet. After double-checking
the ID, I made sure I had the correct
safety deposit box keys from a tin
container, which had also been hidden in
the bottom of the closet. Now I was ready.

WITH LARGE SUNGLASSES covering most of
my face, I entered the bank. I held my
shoulders straight and stood at my full
5'8" and approached the teller.

"I'd like to access my safety deposit
box, please."

The teller took my identification,
studied it and handed it back. "Of course,
Miss Wolf. Let me have you sign your card
first. I'll be right back."

While in the private room, I opened the
box and looked inside. The container was
filled with Ziploc bags, each packed with
$100 bills. There were also several pieces
of expensive jewelry and two more sets of
identifications. A small velvet box held
the diamond ring mother had given me on my

sixteenth birthday. I took it out of the box and slipped it on my right ring finger. The two-carat pink diamond sparkled as I held it up to the light. However, I could not take the chance of wearing it in public. The ring would just call attention to me. I returned it to the box and then tucked in two more bundles of cash from my purse. I snapped the box shut and returned it to its care under the supervision of Bank of America. In another part of town, I did the same thing at a Wells Fargo. While at that bank, I had a teller add $500 to my debit card. I then drove to Citibank, where I purchased a money order for my monthly rent and added another $500 to another debit card. I also put two more packages of cash in the Citibank safety deposit box, a more secure place than the heating vent. Done with my banking, I returned to my small apartment to relax. While it wouldn't make sense to others to have the money spread around town, it made me feel more secure to know not all the money was in one place. Including the money I had placed in several bank accounts in the names of Robin Wolf and Nikki Flowers, I had over 2 million dollars.

On the way up the back steps of my building, I ran into a neighbor, Vicky, a short woman with curly blonde hair and widening hips. Her husband had left her with four small children three years ago. This apartment building was one of the better ones she could afford to rent. Vicky worked as a waitress at the Fremont Hotel and Casino. I liked her. She never complained and always smiled. Today she carried a large basket of dirty clothes as she headed toward the laundry room.

"Hi, Robin" she giggled in her little-girl voice. "How's Nikki?"

I smiled but stayed aloof. She was Nikki's friend and I tried not to interfere with the relationship. "She's fine," I said with a slight Southern accent. "You know, I don't see much of her."

"Well, when you do," she cooed, "tell her I said hello." I smiled and dashed toward my door. Nice, but thank God, not too bright.

☐

FIVE

Current Day

I PUT DOWN THE salad I had been
nibbling on and picked up the book Adam
gave me. The cover of Tattoo History by
Steve *Gilbert was interesting in itself,
with drawings of various tattoos on the
face and body, obviously from the past. The
first chapter displayed several ancient
tattoo tools. Yuk. Hope they didn't use
anything like that today.*

*A five-thousand-year-old frozen body
was discovered on a mountain between
Austria and Italy in October 1991. It made
headlines all over the world. The victim
had apparently been hunting and got caught
in a snowstorm. With his frozen body were
his clothing, a bow, arrows, a bronze ax
and flint for making fire. His skin bore
several tattoos: a cross on the inside of
his left knee, six straight lines above his
kidneys and numerous parallel lines on his
ankles.*

*Instruments that were used for
tattooing during the Upper Paleolithic
(38,000 BC to 10,000 BC) were discovered at
several archaeological sites in Europe.
These instruments consisted of a shallow
bowl, about the size of a medium seashell,
made of clay and red ochre together with
sharp bone needles that were inserted into
the holes in the top of the bowl. The disk
served as a reservoir for the pigment and*

needles were used to pierce the skin.
Tattooed mummies have been found in various
parts of the world. Decorated statuettes
were discovered in Egyptian tombs. All of
the tattooed *Egyptian mummies located to
date have been female.*

*I stopped reading and put the book
down. The lettuce in my bowl was starting
to wilt, so I finished the salad and put
the dishes in the sink. That done, I
returned to my book.*

*Polynesians have been tattooing
themselves for thousands of years. During
early years when Europeans traveled by
ship, they discovered numerous islanders
with tattoos. Tattoos were used as ways of
adorning the body, identifying their
tribes, proclaiming manhood or womanhood.
In Japan, the first written record of
tattooing was found in Chinese dynastic
history of 297 AD. Even American Indians
tattooed themselves. Almost every religion
has tattoos to designate their specific*
beliefs. In Russian prisons, tattoos were
used to show the crime committed and even a
death sentence. In early America, settlers
soon found those with tattoos a curiosity
and we began to see the tattooed lady or
man in the circus.

Whew. I never knew so much about
tattoos. In my school, Our Lady, tattoos
were expressly forbidden, so I hadn't even
considered getting one. A few girls had
gotten tattoos where the nuns would never

see them, but I was never interested. After another four hours of reading and looking at photographs of tattoos of every kind and design, on faces and body parts, it was time to get some sleep.

I put the book down and went to the bathroom to take a shower. In front of the mirror I studied my body. My skin was pale, especially for someone living in the desert, but I had never been much of a sun worshipper. While most of the kids in my high school were soaking up the rays in Aruba or the Cayman Islands, I had been busy plotting my eventual escape by setting up bank accounts and obtaining new identities. Oh, I did my share of partying, but when the others were sleeping off the booze from the night before, I would sneak from the room and work on my plan. Pretending to down drink after drink wasn't too hard, especially when all my underage classmates were too drunk to notice.
Now, looking in the mirror, I had a new appreciation for the art of tattooing, but still didn't relish putting marks on my skin. If I was really going to be a tattoo artist, I knew I would need at least one tattoo. After considering it for several minutes, I decided one small hidden tattoo wouldn't be too bad. I would do it just below my panty line.

SIX

Twelve years ago

EIGHTEEN MONTHS AFTER my father's death, Mom and Carlo were married. A small group of friends joined us in Barbados as I walked Mom down the aisle. Carlo looked handsome in a dark suit and Mom wore a lavender dress. My favorite color, besides Prussian blue, that is. When we returned home, we went straight to a big house in Albany, New York, surrounded by fountains and gardens. I loved the lawns, flowers and trees, but my time in the house was short.

Carlo purchased a loft in Manhattan. I wasn't too happy about being sent to a Catholic school, but I was close to Manhattan apartment and a driver waited for me each afternoon to deliver me to the 10th floor overlooking Central Park. On weekends, we spent time at the estate in Albany.

OUR LADY OF THE Blessed Virgin was a historic building with towers facing the Manhattan skyline. The first day of school, Mom and I took a long black limo to the city. The driver, Jorge, was a thin Mexican with very dark skin. His black eyes were usually hidden behind reflective dark glasses. But when he took his shades off, his eyes reminded me of a spaceman, they were so black. The first day of school, he stopped in front of the old building, opened the door for both of us and then pulled my suitcases out of the trunk. Mom took me by the hand and led me up the steps to the large doors. Inside, I stared at tall ceilings and stained glass that caused an explosion of color on the walls.

Mom leaned over and kissed me on the forehead. "Don't worry, honey. You'll love this school."

I looked up at her. "Why can't I stay with you?"

"Mandy, this is the best school in Manhattan and I will see you every weekend."

A young woman in a habit approached me and reached out her hand. Only slightly taller than me, she had smooth skin, a button nose and lots of freckles. "I'll take you to your room, Amanda."

I looked at my mother and pushed my lips into a pout. But to no avail.

"Amanda, you will love it here. I promise. Besides, Carlo and I will be so busy, we won't be home that often."

I felt my eyes getting wet and looked at my shoes.

"I will see you as often *as I can at the M*anhattan apartment." Mom said. "And, when we can, we'll go to Albany."

Mom gave me one final kiss and walked away with Mother Superior. I carried a small bag, while the tiny nun carried my larger suitcase and led me to my room.

Big girls don't cry! I told myself. But, once alone in my room, hot tears streamed down my face and I muffled my sobs with a pillow from my new bed.

The following Saturday, Jorge arrived to drive me to the apartment. He delivered me to the doorman who loaded me on the elevator and took me up to the penthouse. A short Hispanic woman stood at the door of our apartment, ready to greet me. She wore a crisp, white apron and held a small plate of cookies. She was plump (I was taught never to call people fat) and wore her black hair in braids wrapped around her head. Her face was wide, with large brown eyes and her skin was the color of gingerbread cookies. She held out a plate of sugar cookies.

"Hello, Miss Amanda. I'm Hortencia, your new governess." Her accent was thick, but her voice was melodious and easy to listen to. I followed her.

That weekend, I never saw Mom or Carlo. Angry, I vowed to stay in my room. But after five minutes with Hortencia, I was in love. Hortencia shared stories of her home in Guatemala and taught me words in Spanish for everything in the house. Getting to make tamales was the most fun and I soon started to look forward to my time with her in the kitchen.

For the next several months, my routine consisted of school on Mondays and home on Friday afternoons. On occasion, Jorge would take the long drive to Albany and drop me off at the estate.

Before I knew it, two years had passed and I was ten years old.
⬜

SEVEN

Current Day

ON MONDAY I SHOWED up at the tattoo parlor right at 3:00 p.m. Pamela sat in her usual spot at the counter, chomping on gum and punching keys on her laptop. I smiled as I walked in.

"Hi, Pam. Is Adam in?" Pamela looked up, jerked her head toward the back and returned to her computer screen. I guessed it would take more than a smile to break through that ice. I walked through the parlor, past Pete working on his right arm and peeked into Adam's workroom. I found him intently working on some redhead's butt, the humming needle moving back and forth over her skin. Before I could step back, he looked up.

"Come on in. Jeannie won't mind." The girl on the table nodded, not even bothering to look up.

"If you're sure it's not a problem." I entered the small room and perched on a stool in the corner. Adam put the finishing touches on a small red heart with the name Mark underneath. I sure hoped that was her son or father.

Adam turned off the buzzing needle and the room became silent except for the muted sound of traffic off Fremont. He put the needle aside, carefully cleaned the tattoo on the girl's behind and wiped a small amount of antibacterial cream over the raised reddened area.

"Yes, Jeannie. All done. If it becomes sore just apply some ointment and you'll be fine."

Jeannie sat up on the table; her underpants still down to her pubic hair and twisted her head around, attempting to view her tattooed butt.

"Here." Adam handed her a mirror. "This will make it easier."

Jeannie held it up and her mouth spread into a smile. "Great job, Adam. I'm sure my boyfriend's gonna love it."

So much for that.

When she was gone, Adam turned toward me. "Today, I thought I would give you the tattoo basics."

"Sure, that sounds great."

Adam spent about an hour explaining all the equipment and then reminded me that I needed to get a tattoo. My stomach lurched. Was it really worth it? The desire to be able to create, however, was stronger than my fear of the needle. We agreed that until I decided on a tattoo, I had to experience the needle. So that afternoon, Adam showed me how to prepare a transfer from a drawing and how to apply the transfer to the damp skin. Then he showed me how it felt to be tattooed on my own skin by putting on the transfer and then tattooing without any ink. He used the needle on different parts of my body. Damn, it hurt. I learned that there are parts of the body that are much more sensitive than others, especially where there is less fat or where the skin is close to bones. The skin is especially sensitive in places like the wrists or ankles. I remembered the two young girls in the parlor with the ring around the ankle. Painful!

By the end of the afternoon, I felt I had experienced a thousand bee stings. I had raised red spots on my shoulder, forearm, wrist, breastbone (ouch), and calf and ankle (another ouch). Adam gave me some antiseptic ointment to put on the irritated skin. He told me to pay attention to how the skin healed. Fortunately, for me, he had only done about five to ten pokes with the needle on each spot. Well now I know what a pincushion feels like.

Adam agreed to give me time to design my own tattoo. I went home elated and determined to work on it that evening. I should be special and mean something to me. I indicated that I couldn't have it where my boss could see it. Adam nodded, unaware I lied through my teeth. I never had a job in my life.

EIGHT

New York – Eight year ago

FROM THE WARMTH of my comforter, I
watched as snowflakes swirled around my
bedroom window. Designs stuck against the
glass and then disappeared in the flurries.
I forced myself to leave the comfort of my
bed and got ready for school.

I stepped from the shower, dried myself
off and proudly pulled my new bra out of
the drawer and followed mom's directions. I
pulled the ends to the front under my small
twelve-year-old nubs and hooked the two
ends of the contraption together. After
rotating it, I pushed one arm after another
through the straps and positioned it on my
chest. I finished dressing, stood in front
of the mirror and adjusted the gray skirt
and white blouse. I giggled as I unfastened
the top button of the crisp cotton. From
the drawer, I pulled out the clear gloss,
the only item of makeup I could wear at Our
Lady of the Blessed Virgin and dabbed it on
my pursed lips.

There was a soft knock at my door.

"Miss Amanda," Hortencia's accent
floated through the door. "Your breakfast
is ready."

"Si, Hortencia. Be right there." I
pushed aside the pile of stuffed toys atop

the chest at the foot of my bed and sat down. I pulled on my knee-highs and shoes. My backpack was more difficult to locate. I found it pushed under my bed and soon I slung it over my shoulder and went to the door. The door swung back as I raced out into the hall almost running headlong into Hortencia, who still waited outside.

"Mija," she chided. "slow down." I laughed and took her hand.

At twelve years old, I towered over the five-foot one woman with the raven hair and ebony eyes. A few strands escaped the tight bun at the top of her head. She wore a pale green uniform today, starched and well ironed. A white apron covered her abdomen. I held her hand as we went down the wide curving staircase and back to the kitchen where she and I shared breakfast every morning before school. Mother and Carlo were spending time in the Bahamas after the holidays but would be back any day. Until then I would continue to enjoy my extra time with Hortencia and her stories of life in Mexico.

We sat at the granite countertop in the kitchen, sipping cold fresh-squeezed orange juice. While I nibbled on an omelet, Hortencia talked about her childhood. I had finished my eggs, when Jorge tapped on the kitchen door and stuck his head in. "Miss Amanda, are you ready?" He stole a glance at Hortencia, who picked up the dishes and took them to the sink.

Hortencia rushed me to the foyer, where she dressed me in galoshes, a thick coat, a scarf and mittens. She patted me on the shoulder and directed me toward the door, where Jorge waited impatiently, tapping his fingers against the doorjamb. I turned just in time to see Hortencia lower her lashes and avoid his gaze. Before leaving, I hugged Hortencia and kissed her on the cheek.

Jorge opened the door of the limo and hustled me inside. Once he knew I was safely in, he went around to the driver's door.

"Next stop, señorita, la escuela."
I giggled and snuggled into the rich leather seat.

WHEN MOTHER AND Carlo were in the city, we ate every meal at the large mahogany dining room table. Carlo spoke of current events and often quizzed me about my homework. Mom sipped her wine but was usually quiet when it came to talking about serious issues.

When it was just Hortencia and I, however, we talked about fashion, art, current plays and boys. We giggled and both acted like little girls, but only when we were alone. When Mom and Carlo were present, Hortencia remained professional and serious.

Good grades came easily and I was
considered to be part of the privileged
group. One of those popular girls. We were
often given permission to attend mid-week
plays and concerts, as long as the nannies
were in tow, our parents either too busy
with social events or flying to distant
lands. Then Hortencia and I would dress up
and have Jorge drive us to museums,
Broadway shows and art exhibits.

Weekends, Jorge would pick me up for
the drive upstate where my parents spent
most of their time. Both Hortencia and
Mario, our chef, would already be there
with dinner made. On the estate, I wandered
about, enjoying the freedom and the quiet
away from school and the bustle of the
city. I couldn't complain, but at night I
pulled out the torn drawing of my father
and asked God to keep him safe.

ONE SATURDAY, I WAS exploring the big
house when I decided it was time to ask
Carlo for a horse. My perfect report card
seemed the best negotiation tool, so I
pulled it out of my backpack and quickly
went to his office on the main floor.
Ignoring his rules, I pushed open the large
door and rushed inside. Sitting around the
large table were six men. They stopped
talking and stared at me.

"I'm sorry, Papa." Taking in the
diverse group, I began to back out the
door. There were two men with gray hair,
both with cigars in their mouths. A man in

a dark suit, with slanted eyes and slick black hair, sipped from a large snifter of an amber liquid. Two other men I recognized from other visits to our home and Jorge were also sitting at the table. The most impressive individual was a large black man with a shiny head. Even sitting, he towered over the rest and his arms were huge. I found myself staring.

"Gentlemen," Carlo's voice broke through my reverie. "Can you give me a few moments with my daughter?"

In unison, the men stood and headed toward the door. Jorge winked at me as he passed. But I was too busy watching the large man. The black giant appeared to be wearing football gear on his wide shoulders. When he walked past, he looked down and smiled. His teeth were like a searchlight in the dark of night. When all the men had left the room, I turned toward Carlo, fully expecting a lecture. Instead, he smiled and put out his arms.

"My dear Mandy. What do you need?" I ran to him and he hugged me and ran his large hand over my red hair.

"I'm sorry, Papa. I didn't know you had visitors."

"Just remember to knock," Carlo said.

"Papa," I began. "I wanted to show you my report card." I handed him the card and stood back, a smile on my face.

"Good, good. Another perfect report card. Won't be long and you'll be learning the business."

"Construction business, yuk. I want to be an artist."

Carlo laughed and stroked my head again.

"Papa?"

"Yes, Mandy?"

"May I have a real horse? My pony is getting too small." I rocked back and forth, batting my eyelash at Carlo.

"You are something else," Carlo said. "Sure. We'll get you a horse this summer. Now go and play. I need to finish my business meeting."

"Thank you, Papa," I kissed his cheek, raced out the door past the men, turning only to look once again at the giant. I moved down the hall to the stairs and up to the second story. Making sure my mother or Hortencia were nowhere to be seen, I went to the guest bedroom, right over Carlo's office. I crawled under the bed and slid close to the air vent. As with many old homes, this home still had vents that connected rooms and were perfect places to listen in on conversations. I'd previously discovered this vent while chasing a kitten.

A deep, husky voice, said, "What are we going to do about Taylor?"

"Yes, he is becoming a problem," Carlo responded. "Max, get Roberto to take care of it."

Roberto was one of Carlo's men. He was small in stature, with bad skin and straight black hair, worn in a ponytail. He delivered messages to Carlo, telling Jorge what to do, and would leer at Mom and Hortencia when Carlo wasn't looking. A skinny Puerto Rican, Roberto had greasy hair and a pencil-thin mustache. He gave me the creeps.

"Yes, sir. I'll see that it's taken care of." The unfamiliar voice boomed through the vent. I knew it had to be the giant.

"Miss Amanda!" Hortencia's voice sounded far off. She was probably calling me for lunch. I wriggled away from the vent and out from under the bed. I ran down the main staircase. Curious, I wondered who Taylor was and how Roberto was going to take care of him?

NINE

Las Vegas - Current Day

THE SOUND OF MOZART interrupted my
dream. I yawned and stretched awake. Today
I needed to take a trip. I got up slowly,
thinking about the tattoo idea running
through my head. I looked at the clock. It
was early, so I took out a pad and began to
make some sketches before going out.

I showered, taking my time. I was
delaying the inevitable but dreaded going
out. I sat in my robe and looked at the pad
in front of me. With pencil in hand, I put
the tattoo I'd dreamed of on paper.

For my tattoo I decided on a simple
monogram of ANR. I stood and looked down at
the design. Satisfied, I closed the drawing
pad and went to the bathroom. I had delayed
enough.

I pulled out Robin's ID and put Nikki's
information in the back of the closet. When
the blond wig was atop my head, I tied it
back into a ponytail and applied my makeup.
My clothing today would be casual. I put on
a pair of worn jeans, a cotton blouse and
sandals. I checked my purse, grabbed
another set of keys and headed out the
door.

The drive to the parking structure where I had three reserved spaces in three different names, took about 10 minutes. I pulled the red Toyota into a space between Robin's Highlander and a 1995 Oldsmobile. For the next half hour, I sat with all three cars running to keep the batteries charged, and then I locked up the two Toyotas and jumped into the Olds.

The ride down the I-515 to the Henderson Public Library took less than hour. On a weekday afternoon, there was plenty of parking in the lot. I left the car in one of the farthest spaces and went into the library. I kept the large sunglasses on and went straight back to the computers. There were plenty of unused terminals. I selected one facing away from any library patrons and typed in Carlo Rinaldi. I cringed at the long list of hits.

There were the usual reports of Rinaldi Construction building another skyscraper and older hits discussing his suspected criminal activities. I scrolled down the list until I found what I was looking for. Another article detailed the search for Carlo Rinaldi's beloved stepdaughter, Amanda Nicole Rinaldi. One photo showed Carlo standing in front of one of his buildings. My mother stood next to him. Even in the grainy black and white photograph, her face appeared haggard. Both were dressed in expensive clothing. Carlo's once handsome face was now heavy with the

years of a too extravagant life. My
mother's diamonds gleamed.

Another article detailed the
disappearance of seventeen-year old Amanda
on the day of her graduation from a private
school in Manhattan over two years ago. The
suspected kidnapping was not discovered
until one week later, when she didn't show
up for a summer course at Parson's Paris
School of Art and Design in France. No
ransom call was ever made. At least as far
as the police knew. There were rumors of
large amounts of cash missing from the
Rinaldi home, but Carlo disputed this
claim. Then two weeks after Amanda's
disappearance, her purse with all her
credit cards, identification, traveler's
checks and a blood-soaked scarf were found
on a beach in Miami. The article concluded
with comments from the distraught parents
offering $50,000 for information leading to
the whereabouts of Amanda or those who had
taken her.

I thought the trip to Florida in an old
car I had bought from some Rican for cash
under an assumed name was a clever ruse.
The cut on my thigh provided the blood for
the scarf and leaving over $1,000 in
traveler's checks would make anyone think I
had been the victim of foul play. The
reward bothered me slightly. I knew that
Carlo would stop at nothing to find me or
his money.

The screen showed another story of interest. I clicked twice and a color photo of Carlo and my mom filled the screen. A small commentary at the bottom indicated that they attended a fundraiser for a Senator in her quest for the presidency. I laughed silently. It really was true that she would take money from any criminal in her efforts to get back into the White House. I turned my attention back to the screen. Carlo was gaining weight. His belly strained at the tuxedo jacket and he appeared to be getting jowls. I was surprised to see how much gray was now in his formerly jet-black hair. This photograph was better, but my mother still looked tired. Her red hair appeared dull and her face drawn. Her eyes were the most telling. She had a look of defeat. I reached out and touched the screen. I wanted to let her know I was alive, but mom had long ago stopped caring about anything. No longer was she the vivacious woman I remembered before my father's death. She appeared like a robot. She attended her charity functions, stood next to Carlo and rested her bejeweled hand on his expensive sleeve. Meanwhile, he continued to work his way into the political arena. But I knew about my mother's midnight forays to the liquor cabinet to drown her sorrow.

I clicked on a link and watched as Chief Foley spoke. I remembered her from my childhood. Foley still had the soft chocolate-brown eyes, but now had slivers of gray at her temples. Mother stood

silently behind her. The Chief told how the
New York Police Department would not stop
until my disappearance was solved. The
interview concluded with more information
on the reward being offered for information
leading to a solution in this case.

I took a gulp of air. No one in the
library took notice. I wanted to click off
the computer and run, but I spent the next
half hour reading through numerous
unrelated categories to erase as much as
possible of my recent searches. I hit the
backspace and returned to the Google list.
I did my best to clear the history. Then I
turned off the computer, took out a wipe
and cleaned off the mouse, screen and
keyboard. Only then did I get up and leave
the library. I drove to a small park near
the library and parked away from the
softball field. Under a tree, I sobbed. How
would God forgive me for my lies? When done
crying and feeling sorry for myself, I
switched on the engine and left the park.

On the highway headed back to Vegas, I
drove mechanically. I hated Carlo. I
couldn't believe that I had once called him
"Dad."

In the parking structure, I switched
back to my red Toyota and returned to the
apartment. When I had locked the door
behind me, I let the tears flow once again.
I spent the next two hours mired in my own
loneliness and wondered if the revenge had
been worth it. Then I dried my tears and

dabbed my swollen eyes with a chilled
washcloth. Time to get back to reality.

TEN

New York - Seven Years Ago

I STOOD IN MY bedroom, hidden by the curtain and watched as several limos drove through the estate gates and toward the house. Teens spilled from luxury cars and hastened to the large tents erected on the South lawn. Today was my thirteenth birthday party.

"Mija," Hortencia called. "Let me finish your hair." I took one last look as a white limousine parked and a valet opened the door. A woman reached out a hand, covered with jewels, and a valet helped her from the car. Her gown sparkled in the spotlights that illuminated the gardens.

"Si, mi amiga," I said to Hortencia. I closed the curtains and turned. "Make me beautiful."

"Yes, sweetheart." Hortencia laughed and patted the chair in front of my vanity. I sat and looked into the mirror. Hortencia picked up the brush and ran it through my shoulder length red hair. She pulled back my hair and pinned it up on the sides. Finally, she placed a small bouquet of white flowers to one side.

"Hortencia, can I put on some makeup?"

"Mija, you are only thirteen. You are almost a lady, but not quite. How about a little lip gloss?"

"Alright." My mother would easily have caved, but Hortencia kept me in line. I knew she loved me, so I let her. I picked up the gloss and dabbed a little on my lips.

"Enough." Hortencia put down the brush and stood back. "Let me look at you."

I stood and twirled.

"How pretty you look."

In front of the full-length mirror I looked at myself. Since last year, I had grown and was now 5 feet 6 inches tall. The emerald silk dress complimented my red hair and made my green eyes sparkle.

I threw my arms around Hortencia and gave her a quick kiss on the cheek. Her face reddened and she pushed me away.

"Now go," she giggled and began straightening items on my vanity. I turned and left the room.

I MADE MY ENTRANCE just as Carlo mounted the podium and picked up the microphone. My mother stood quietly by his side.

"Good evening, everyone. Tonight, we celebrate my lovely daughter's thirteenth birthday. Mandy, come up here."

I left my best friend, Susan, and stepped on the stage to stand beside Carlo. He placed his arm around my shoulder and pulled me close.

Carlo cleared his throat. "This is indeed special and to start the evening, I want to present my dear Mandy with a unique gift."

I looked down at the over two hundred guests and wondered what could be more special than this large celebration.

"Jose, bring it out." Carlo bellowed into the microphone.

From what I thought had just been another serving tent, Roberto lifted the flap and exposed a new sports car.

"Oh, my God." I said. I turned to Carlo and hugged him. He took me in his arms. He held me a little too long and much too tightly. I felt his warmth through my thin dress. I looked at my mother as her eyes shifted away. I quickly pecked Carlo on the cheek and pulled away.

"Thank you, thank you," I said a little too loudly. I turned and started toward the shiny, red car. Carlo grabbed my upper arm and pulled me back.

"Later," he said. "Jose. Garage."
Speaking into the microphone, he said, "And
now, more celebration."

Music played. Slowly a voice began to
sing Happy Birthday. I turned to look at
the opposite stage. Britney Spears stepped
out of the shadows and a spotlight hit her.
The crowd roared as she sang the first
words of the song. She was about to say my
name when a male voice chimed in. The
onlookers screamed as Justin Timberlake
came onto the stage. The crowd sang along.

I ran down from the stage and joined
Susan. Together we danced. We ignored the
boys who attempted to get us to dance.
After a few hours, I could no longer stand
the crowd. When Susan spotted Tommy Harris,
a local jock, and wanted to make contact, I
slunk into the crowd and disappeared toward
the garage. I ran my hand over the candy-
red paint and admired the white leather.

I knew I'd better get back to the
guests. But first I wanted to go to my room
and check on the chinchilla Persian kitten
my mother had bought me the last month.

I slipped past the partiers, snuck
along the side of the house and entered the
house through the servant's entrance. With
all the excitement in the kitchen, the
cooks and servers never even noticed as I
slid past them and up the back stairs. I
moved down the upstairs hallway toward my

bedroom, when I spotted the white ball of
fur run into one of the guestrooms. I
followed him in just as his tail
disappeared under the bed. I got down on my
hands and knees to retrieve him and heard
voices drift up from the floor vent.
Curious, I flattened myself and scooted
under the bed.

    "Max, get the Senator a drink."
Carlo's voice commanded.

    "Yes, sir." Max's baritone voice boomed
through the vent. Max was now a constant in
our lives and I had come to love this
gentle giant who provided security to
Carlo. But I still didn't trust him.

    "Gentlemen, let's get started."

    I listened as chairs were pulled across
the marble floors. The murmur of voices
droned on for several minutes and then it
became silent. Carlo's voice took command
of the group.

    "The unions have finally consented to
work with us. The Senator has made an
agreement to push for unionization of the
hotel employees when we are done with the
building, as long as the unions leave
Rinaldi Construction out of the equation.
The Teamsters will take over with our
assistance and receive the city contracts
on maintenance and trash. We will be able
to import our labor on H-1 visas with no
interference."

"However," an unfamiliar voice added, "We are getting resistance from Senator Gomez. He wants unionization of all construction in the state. He's been pushing this agenda for years. We have offered to assist him with his election next year, but he wants to make sure his people are taken care of and wants to keep immigrants out of the picture."

Another voice added, "He's also trying to pass other legislation that will raise taxes on big business. His agenda is to provide additional support to the Hispanics already in the city."

The voices droned and I found myself starting to doze. Just as I was about to scoot out from under the bed, Carlo's voice increased in volume.

"He's becoming a problem. I'm concerned he will do whatever he can to push his own agenda and interfere with Manhattan West. We can't afford that. This is a five hundred-million-dollar project and we cannot have him messing it up."

Several voices agreed.

"It's time to fix the problem. Max, notify Roberto."

Yuk! I thought. Not that slimy Roberto again. Tired, I crawled from under the bed and returned to the party. I danced with

Britney and Justin on the stage. When Marshall Southwick approached me for a dance, I begged off and went back to Susan and danced some more. When the party finally broke up, I returned to my room and spent hours drawing my new car. Dawn peaked through the curtains when I put down my drawing pad and finally fell asleep.

A MONTH LATER, I was back in the city spending more and more time at Our Lady, coming to the estate only on weekends. Carlo was busy with a big project in Washington, D.C. and mother spent more and more time either in her room or at some charity event. Then one weekend when I was alone with Hortencia, I found her staring at the newspaper when I came down for breakfast. She appeared to be crying.

"What's wrong, Hortencia?" I asked.

"Senator Gomez died in an accident," she explained.

"Senator Gomez?"

"Yes, my uncle met him last year. Good man. He was trying to help our people," she wiped at her eyes.

"What happened?"

"He and his wife were killed in a car accident. The papers say he was drinking and drove over a cliff."

"Oh," I said. Senator Gomez? Then I remembered Carlo's comment about Roberto fixing the problem.

I recalled the conversation among my father's mob and turned to Hortencia. "What is an H-1 Visa?"

"Oh," she sniffled again. "Where did you hear that?"

"Just some friends talking. But I didn't understand what they were talking about."

"It was something Senator Gomez was against. It is just a way for business owners to get cheap labor from other countries."

"How does it work?" I asked.

"Well," she continued. "A business can bring in someone from a foreign country when they say they cannot find someone to do the work here. They then pay them less than they would Americans. Mexicans are one of the few who never seem to get these visas. Usually they come from Asia, China or the Middle East. Also, once they get here, they never leave. But no one talks about the thousands that do this. They only talk about the illegal Mexicans."

"Oh," I said, still curious about the connection between Carlo, Roberto and Senator Gomez.

ELEVEN

Current Day

IT WAS HOT ENOUGH to bake cookies on the sidewalk when I entered the coolness of the parlor. I had already done several tattoos, mostly of flowers and hearts on the butts of young girls and names across the biceps of young men. I suspected most would likely be back in a tattoo parlor in a month or so looking to modify or cover it.

One Wednesday around the end of May, I walked in and received the typical glare from gum-popping Pamela. I peeked through the beaded curtain, where Adam was alone working on a design.

"Here," I said, "handing him a transfer. This is my tattoo."

"What did you decide on?" He asked looking up at me.

"My own design. I've already made up the transfer."

Adam took the design, looked at it and then looked at me with furrowed brows.

ANR

"ANR, huh. That a boyfriend or something?" he asked.

"ANR?" I turned toward the voice to see Pam standing behind me.

"No, I don't have a boyfriend," I said and turned back to Adam. "It's an old friend. I know it won't make sense to anyone else, but my friend was very special to me."

Adam pursed his lips and nodded. "Hey, you got it. It is kind of plain though. Where do you want it?"

My face reddened. "Well," I said. "I can't really have any tattoos showing because of my job. I was thinking on my hip." I avoided looking at him. Pam sat down on a stool in the corner.

"Okay," he sighed. "We'll have to figure out what to do about that. A lot of people are uncomfortable about having someone tattoo them if they don't sport a tattoo themselves. But this is a start. Do you have an idea of the color?"

"Um, sorry. I didn't think about color or anything else when I put it together. Maybe a soft brown? And, can you put a couple of small leaves on it?" Having Pam watch this exchange made me even more nervous. I glanced at her.

"You got it. I'll make it nice and discrete." He looked up at Pam. "Who's watching the front desk?"

"Your friend, Carlos, came in for another tat." I stiffened at the name and Pam stared at me for several seconds.

"Carlos? Hey if that guy wants another tattoo, he'll need this room. The only places he has left on his body requires privacy." Adam chuckled.

Pam shrugged. "You have time. They're just going over ideas now." She turned to me. "I'll give you two some privacy and let you know when they are ready."

After she left, I unzipped my black jeans and opened them slightly. Adam laughed.

"You're going to have to pull the pants down further than that. Why don't you take off the pants and you can just pull your panties down to your hips?" He reached over and grabbed a towel and handed it to me.

After I undressed and lay on the table, with Adam turned the other way, he took the transfer and began to prep my skin. First, he put on a pair of surgical gloves. Then he carefully wiped the area with alcohol. He took a new Bic shaver and ran it over the area to remove excess body hair. When satisfied, he spread a thin layer of petroleum jelly on my skin and reached for the transfer. Like carbon paper, the transfer had been made from tracing my original drawing on the back side of the carbon. When he placed it on my skin, the drawing transferred easily onto my skin.

"What does it mean?" he asked again.

"Someday, I promise, I'll tell you."

"Deal. Are you ready? This is gonna hurt."

I knew that already.

"I'm ready," I said in a more confident tone. No, I wasn't scared. Adam had shown me how it felt to get tattooed. I loved him for it. He wasn't forcing me to get a tattoo, but we both knew I needed to have at least one tattoo to be a real tattoo artist.

As Adam readied the needle and inks, I began to think about who I was. Was I really Amanda Nicole Rinaldi? No! I was Amanda Nicole Bartoli. My father was Michael Bartoli. I sat up quickly, startling Adam. "Stop!"

"You're not going to back out, now are you?"

"No." I said stepping off the table. "I just need to make a change to the drawing."

Adam looked at me, one eyebrow raised. "Okay."

I picked up the drawing and made a few corrections and prepared a new transfer. When done, I handed it over to Adam. "The is the correct one."

He looked at the new monogram. "I'm not even going to ask."

I looked at the new drawing and smiled. *Yes. This was the correct one.*

"I forgot that my friend got married. These are her new initials."

Adam smiled and picked up the needle. "You still want me to add some ivy leaves?"

"Please."

Then the needle buzzed and I felt tingling as it traced the up and down movements of my drawing.

About fifteen minutes later, I looked at the one inch high by two-inch long tattoo on my now irritated skin. It appeared rather plain compared to the tattoos usually done in the parlor. I got up from the table and stood before the full-length mirror, looked at the tattoo and smiled. I stared in the mirror for a few minutes and then turned to Adam.

He looked at it, looked up at me and nodded. I jumped back up on the table and endured the preparation and the few minutes it took him to add the small modification. When he was done, I once again looked at the small tattoo and smiled. Now it was right. ANB. Amanda Nicole Bartoli. B felt more like it. Michael Bartoli was my father, not Carlo. That was who I really was.

"Done." Adam said.

I smiled at him and started to pull up my pants.

"Can I see?"

Pam came up behind me, startling me again.

"Sure," I said feeling the heat in my face. I pulled my pants back down and lifted the small gauze strip covering the fresh tattoo. Pam leaned close and studied it.

"That looks different," she stood and looked in my eyes. "You sure it's not a boyfriend?"

"No, just an old friend." I put the bandage back in place and pulled up my pants. When I turned, Pam was gone.

"Thanks, Adam."

Adam and I walked out of the back room. When I reached the front desk, Pam smiled at me. Confused, I returned the smile and went to the sitting area where two young girls were looking through a tattoo book. I sat across from them with my back to the door.

"What are you looking for?" I asked. Both girls appeared quite young and I vowed to check their IDs before I tattooed them. The girl on the left was very overweight, which would make it easy to tattoo her. She had bright red hair and tons of freckles. One half of her head was shaved close and the other side with hair down to her shoulders. She wore excessive makeup and bright red lipstick. Who was I to talk, with my overly-painted eyes and almost black lipstick. I moved over to look at the other girl. In contrast to the first girl, this one was extremely thin, which would make tattooing more painful. (Since her bones much closer to the skin.) This girl's makeup was scant and her long, honey blonde hair was pulled up in a ponytail. They were positively an odd couple.

"We're thinking about getting small tattoos on our ankles." The redhead said.

I learned forward and was about to say something when the old cowbell over the door clanked. The two girls stopped going through the tattoos and stared over my shoulder. I looked up and Pamela's face lit up. Slowly, I turned around.

Backlit by the light from the street stood a tall man of about 6'2" or 6'3". As he moved further into the parlor, I almost gasped. He had dark brown hair and even in the dim light of the parlor, I could see his golden-brown eyes. Large dimples cratered his cheeks dusted with a sparse beard. He looked like a young Tom Selleck in his Marlboro days. All he needed were boots and a hat. I fully expected a horse to come trotting in behind him. I tried not to stare as he smiled at Pamela, who left her desk and ran to the stranger. He picked up all 5'10" feet of her without effort and swung her around.

"Hey, Adam," the visitor said in a loud voice as he put Pam down. Adam now stood at the back of the parlor, with a shocked look on his face.

"I'll be a son of a gun," Adam said. He stepped forward and the two embraced. I noticed the stranger almost lifted Adam off the floor and he was no lightweight. "Are you really here?"

"My God, man. I wasn't sure I'd ever see you again." Adam said when he finally let go. Pam no longer chewed gum, which she probably stuck under the counter. She grinned.

"Glad you're home," Pam said as the man leaned down and planted another kiss on the top of her pink and blonde head.

"Hey, where are *my manners?"* Adam said. *He grabbed* the stranger's arm and turned him towards me. "Jerry, this is Nikki. She's been working with us for a few months now. Got some real talent."

"Glad to meet you," I stood and I offered my hand. The two girls stared without shame.
"Wow, manners and everything," he said. His laugh filled the room. "If you're a friend of Adam's and Pam's, you're a friend of mine." He wrapped his arms around me and pulled me into a hug. Boy, this guy really likes hugging.

I could have stayed there for a year, but I felt my body respond and pulled away. It had been a long time since I had even had male contact, and, let's face it, any girl would want contact with this guy.

Adam interrupted. "You back for good now?"

"Yep. My tour's over." I sat again and pretended to be working on a drawing, but when I looked up, Jerry was watching me. I totally forgot the two girls sitting on the sofa.

"Do you have a place to stay?" Pam asked.

"Sure. I'm back in my place. The guy leasing it re-upped. Not me, though. Two tours were enough."

"Were you in Afghanistan?" I asked.

"Yep," he saluted. "And proud of it. Kicked some ass over there and helped a lot of people, but now it's time to get my life back."

"Alright," Pam said. "You gonna show us?"
I wasn't sure what she was talking. Then Jerry unbuttoned his shirtsleeve and started to roll up his sleeve.

"Just like I wrote. Here it is."

Pam and Adam looked on while Jerry displayed a bulging bicep with the earth, an anchor and an eagle. US Marine Corp was written below the tattoo.

"Not bad," Adam offered. "Too bad you didn't let me do it."

"Don't feel bad. You get to do the big one and I have a great idea of what I want."

"Okay, but how about we close up shop and all go to dinner," Adam said and then noticed the two girls still staring at Jerry. "Hey, did you girls pick out something?"

The dark-haired girl pulled her eyes away from Jerry and looked at Adam.

"Can we come back tomorrow?"

"Sure," Adam said. He pulled out a small sample book and handed it to the redhead. "Take this and look through it."

When they left, Adam turned off lights and I packed up my stuff while the three of them prepared to close shop. Jerry approached me and smiled.

"You coming with us? Nikki, isn't it?"

"That's okay," I lowered my eyes. "You go. I'm sure you have lots to catch up on."

"Wouldn't hear of it," Jerry said. "You're coming with us."

We left our cars in the parking lot and walked the few blocks to the strip. It felt great to get out for a change. I enjoyed the lights and the excitement of the strip. We selected a cheap buffet and waited next to flashing lights and ringing bells for our table. The smell of alcohol floated through the air and reminded me that the ID I had showed at the door for Nikki Flowers was a fake. I still had months to go before reaching my twenty-first birthday.

When Adam and Jerry ordered beer and Pamela a strawberry margarita, I didn't dare push it. I ordered a cola. We stuffed ourselves with mediocre salads and fried chicken. A couple of times during the meal Pamela raised the right side of her mouth and closed her right eye in a smirk. I ignored it. She chattered away, asking

Jerry all about his time in Afghanistan. I listened intently, enjoying the company of my new friends. Especially Jerry. He sat close and I found his body heat exciting. After dinner and some turns at a five-cent poker machine, we headed back to our cars. Pamela and Adam seemed in a hurry to get home and said their goodbyes and jumped in their car, leaving Jerry and I standing in the parking lot. Jerry walked me to my car and made sure I was safely inside. He tapped on the window just after I started the motor. I lowered the window and looked up at him.

"I hope I see you again," he said and smiled. His straight white teeth glistened in the overhead lights.

"Me too." I hoped he didn't see the blush traveling up my neck. I raised the window, smiled and backed out of the lot. My heart pounded loudly in my chest and I barely made my way back to my apartment. □

TWELVE

New York - Five Years Ago

"DAMN."

I lay on my back half under the
guestroom bed. Claustrophobia overcame me
and it was difficult to breathe. At
fifteen, my body was no longer that of a
skinny pre-teen and my nose now touched the
wooden slats of the bed frame. I pushed at
the floor and attempted to get closer to
the air vent hidden under the head of the
bed. My tennis shoes squeaked against the
wood floor. I stopped, listened. Nothing.
Whew, I was safe. Now, my maturing body fit
only part way, unable to reach the opening.
I waited, trying to think. Frustrated, I
slid from my hiding place and sat up.

I'd learned much about Carlo's illegal
activities while listening at the vent. I
listened while the men talked about
payoffs, extortion, illegal union
activities and corrupt politicians
throughout New York State. But today my
curiosity was piqued. From my bedroom
window, I could see four black cars
carrying men I had not seen before. Luxury
sedans arrived. Several of Carlo's men
drove onto the property and parked in the
back the house.

I was still sitting on the floor
pondering what to do, when Hortencia's
voice floated down the hall.

"Amanda, are you up there?" Hortencia opened and closed doors, moving down the hall. I got up from the floor and slipped into the bathroom adjacent to the guest room. Just seconds later, the bedroom door opened.

"Amanda?" There was a pause, then Hortencia closed the door.

Hortencia's footsteps faded away. I stayed hidden. I couldn't chance losing my secret spot. The vent was a perfect place to keep up on Carlo's activities, but not if I could no longer squeeze into the space. I tried to think of a solution.

I ran down the hall to my room. I knelt at the cedar chest at the end of my bed and pulled out an artist's pad and a box of colored pencils, put them on the vanity and started to draw. My hand traveled back and forth across the pad. I changed pencils frequently. A strange tingling sensation journeyed up from my toes to my fingers. I shook it off and continued to focus onmy project. I flipped the page and started a new drawing. A shiver traveled down my spine and before I knew it, the drawings were done. Only twenty minutes had passed. The three drawings consisted of my bedroom, the guestroom, and Hortencia's room, all in detail. I leaned back. Never having had an art class, I was amazed at my own skills. Each drawing boasted new furniture and curtains. In the guestroom, a large, four-poster bed offered a higher clearance from the floor, perfect for me to slip under and listen.

Satisfied, I picked up my illustrations and went toward Mother's room.

Propped on a pile of silk pillows, Mother held a romance novel in her left hand and a tall glass of amber liquid in her right. A crystal decanter, its stopper lying on the nightstand, confirmed my mother was drinking in the late morning.

"Mom," I said, a tinge of defiance in my voice. "I'm tired of all the pink in my bedroom. Would you be comfortable with me redecorating it?"

Kathryne nodded.

"Also, would you approve of me redoing the upstairs guestroom?"

"Sure, honey, just make sure your father approves." Mother turned back to her book.

I knew Mother would consent. She deferred to Carlo for everything these days. It often made me angry, but I would work things to my advantage. Since Carlo was not in the least interested in household affairs, I knew this one would be a slam-dunk. It also gave me an excuse to see who was in the meeting going on downstairs.

I hurried down the stairs to the large mahogany doors of Carlo's office and knocked.

"Yes?" Carlo sounded irritated.

I opened the door and stuck my head inside. A dozen men sat around the large table; smoke spiraling from their ashtrays. Carlo sat at the head of the table with the black giant, Max, on his right side. The two Hispanics, Roberto and Jorge, were on the right. Chan, the Chinese also sat on the right side. Having listened to Carlo's meetings numerous times from my secret perch upstairs, I picked out Serge, the Russian, Gianni and Milano, the two Italians, and a new bodyguard, Winston, the Samoan. One thing I could say about Carlo, he was an equal opportunity mobster. Besides the usual crew, there were a couple of others I didn't recognize.

Carlo turned, smiled and motioned me over. "Mandy," he said. "What can I do for you?" As he often did, he ran his hand down my long red hair.

"Papa?" I lowered my lashes. "Mom said I could do some redecorating of the rooms upstairs and I wanted to see if Jorge could take me downtown to pick out some new furniture?"

Amanda smiled and Carlo nodded. "Sure, Mandy." He placed his hand on my arm and I withheld a shudder. "However, I think

I would prefer that Max take you. You are getting too old to be out there without protection."

I *frowned but said nothing. It was* possible to get away with anything with Jorge. He often talked to his bookie while I did whatever I wanted. But who was Max? The giant of a black man with the baldhead and acne scars on his cheeks was a stranger.

Max stood, towering over everyone. I shivered and looked up at him. For some reason, of all Carlo's men, Max frightened me the most. He turned toward me. His mouth spread into a smile and I noticed the sparkle of a diamond-stud in his unusually white smile. He had a diamond in his tooth? He excused himself from the table and walked toward the door. The floor shook when he walked.

"I didn't mean right now," I said and backed away from the giant.

"Go," Carlo said, again touching my bare arm. "It will do you some good to get out of the house." He nodded at Max.

Silently, I followed Max out of the study, trying to figure out my next step.

"I need to run up and get my purse and decorating ideas," I rushed up the stairs. In my room, I pulled out my cell phone and punched in a number. I waited impatiently while the phone rang.

"Hello?" A voice responded.

"Sam, it's me. Can you call your friend for me?"

"Sure."

"Ask him to meet me inside the first furniture store on the right of the Lexington Design Center, next to the main entrance. Have him wait back by the bathrooms. Tell him I'll be there in about an hour. Does he have the ID? Okay, thanks." I hit "end" and picked up my purse. With drawings in hand, I rushed down the stairs.

Max waited in the foyer, his hands behind his back and legs spread slightly. When I reached the bottom of the stairs, he went to the front door and opened it. The Lincoln was already waiting. Once seated in back, I leaned forward.

"I'd like to go to the Design Center on Lexington, please."

"Yes, ma'am. I think it's 200 Lexington," he responded and sped off.

Twenty minutes later, we entered the Design Center. In the main furniture room, I traveled from display to display, selecting furniture. I kept an eye on the time and when it was time, I turned to Max.

"I'm going to the powder room," I
stated and went to the hallway at the back
of the store.

I checked on Max. He remained where he
was. I snuck into the bathroom and waited.
Nothing. I tapped lightly on the men's room
door. A young man, wearing a hooded
sweatshirt and faded jeans peeked out.

"You Mandy?"

I nodded.

"Got your stuff. You got the money?"

"Of course." I reached into her purse
and pulled out an envelope. I looked toward
the showroom. No Max.

He looked in the envelope and quickly
counted the money. He stuffed the envelope
in his sweatshirt.

"It's all there. Four hundred. Is the
ID good?" I took the package from him and
stuffed it into her handbag.

"Good as you can get. Let me know when
you want more."

He retreated into the restroom. I took
the envelope and went into the women's
restroom. Once inside I inspected the
contents. The photo was definitely me, but
older. I confirmed the name on the birth

certificate matched both the social security card and the driver's license. Satisfied, I shoved them all into my purse and left the restroom. I almost ran headlong into Max. He stood at the end of the hall in his typical stance, legs spread, and hands behind his back.

"Ready to finish the order?" Max asked. I gave a quick nod and moved past him, feeling the blood rise to my cheeks. At the counter, I turned to ask him a question. He was nowhere to be seen. I trembled when Max exited the restroom aisle, wiping his hands.

He approached me and pulled out the credit card he had been given by Carlo. When Max was about to pay, I looked back toward the restrooms and noticed a four-poster bed off the right. It was the bed. I stepped away from Max and walked toward the display. I pulled the drawing from my purse and was shocked to see the bed was an exact replica of my drawing in every detail. In fact, the entire layout matched.

"This is the bed I drew," I told Max. Without thinking, I gave it to Max.

"You sure?" He took the drawing and looked at me, his eyebrows arched.

"Yes, this is the bed I want."

They made the changes to the order and Max turned to me with an odd smile on his face.

"Are you done now?"
"Yes."

When the salesperson handed him the invoice, he didn't even blink. He gave him the credit card, signed and made delivery arrangements.

"I'm starving," I said, "Can we stop at the food court for a sandwich?"

"No problem," he responded. "Where would you like to go?"

"Anywhere is fine."

We walked in silence to the food court and I ordered a sandwich and bottled water and then turned to Max.

"Would you like something?"

"No, thank you," he said. "I'll wait until we return."

I took my purchase and headed toward the parking area. Max lumbered behind me. A homeless man in a torn overcoat approached us. He held an empty Styrofoam coffee cup in one hand.

"Can I have …" he began, but Max quickly stepped in his path.

Startled by the sudden appearance of the homeless man, I was slow to react. Max, however, pulled out five dollars and stuffed it into the man's outstretched hand.

The man walked away. I looked up at Max surprised but said nothing.

THREE WEEKS LATER, my old furniture was donated to a local charity and a brand-new mahogany bed, with plenty of space underneath sat in front of my secret vent. That day, I heard Carlo talking to Max alone.

"Max, I want you to take over driving Amanda. I don't want anything to happen to her. She means a lot to me."

"Yes, sir," Max's deep voice boomed through the vent.

"Someday that girl will *be a part of this operation."* Carlo confided. "Unlike her mother, she's got a head on her shoulders. I'll get her into Harvard and she'll bring some respectability to Rinaldi Construction. Little charmer, but I don't want some asshole coming near her. You keep an eye out. Got it?"

"Yes, sir."

Carlo continued to ramble. "When I first met her mother, I knew she had to be mine. Roberto took care of that for me.

Well, now I got her and she's turning into a lush. I won't let that happen to Amanda. You see to it that no*thing happens to* her."

What? What did Roberto take care of? I wanted to scream. Now I knew that Carlo had killed my father and there was nothing I could do. Or was there? I needed time to plan. In the meantime, I would play the role of the dutiful daughter. My blood boiled, but I took a few deep breaths and then crawled out from under the bed. I continued to work on my plan, listening to Carlo and his men regularly whenever I was at the estate. I looked at the bed, straightened the bed skirt, turned and left the guest room with a smirk on my face. I'll get you yet! I promised.
□

THIRTEEN

Current Day

IT WAS ANOTHER sweltering day at the shop. Pete had packed up his tools and left an hour before to attend his son's birthday party. Though it was my regularly scheduled day at the shop, I visited more often. Both Adam and Pam seemed to accept my explanation of extra vacations days from the casino.

Today, I worked on some designs for temporary tattoos. I relished the idea of creating art that was not permanent. To me, paintings should be able to be moved, shared, updated. Having a tattoo as a lasting piece of art on my body didn't excite me. The small piece on my stomach would be a reminder of my father, so I could live with that. Adam came from the back and sat next to me.

"Whatcha doing?"

"Working on some ideas for temporary tattoos. I was doing some research and found that you can sell a lot of them to people who aren't sure what they want or to kids who just want to wear them for a party and remove them the next day or so."

Adam took my pad and paged through the drawings. "These are pretty good." He looked over his shoulder. "What do you think, Pam?"

Pam raised her head when Adam held up the pad to show her a few of the drawings. "I think it's a good idea."

Ah, kudos from Pam.

At six p.m., Adam and I were in the process of straightening up the shop when Jerry entered and invited us to his home for dinner. Without a word, Pam shut down her computer, packed it in its case and threw it over her shoulder.

"Come on, guys. Hurry it up." She stood next to Jerry, her hands on her hips. Adam and I finished closing and followed Jerry and Pam out the door. I decided to take my own car to Jerry's home. He gave me the address in North Vegas, just in case I lost them while enroute. Both cars were easy to follow until Adam motioned me to keep following Jerry and turned off into a strip mall.

I followed Jerry to a nice housing complex and he made sure to get me through the guard gate. We drove past two-story units with palm lined roads, pools, etc. He directed me to park in a guest slot next to his garage and led me into his place. He apologized for the mess and told me he had only had a little time to clean up after the previous renter. But the place was neat and well furnished. The living room was large with high ceilings. A moderate-sized patio faced out onto a common area landscaped with a dry creek bed and cacti.

Beyond the creek bed I could see desert leading up to hills. Jerry gave me a tour of the upstairs. The master bedroom was tastefully decorated with a king size bed and a matching cherry wood dresser. *An open Bible lay* on the nightstand. I felt uncomfortable standing at the bedroom door, I followed Jerry back to the kitchen where he pulled a beer from the refrigerator and offered it to me. I shook my head.

"Sorry, I forgot you don't drink. Would you like a soda?"

Just then Pam and Adam walked in. Their arms were loaded with pizza, beer and more soda for me.

In the living room, Jerry told us of his time in Afghanistan, not going into any gory details. Adam brought Jerry up to date on how the business was doing. Several times I caught Pam looking at me. What is up with that? After eleven p.m., I excused myself from the reunion and said my goodbyes. I headed for my car. From his doorway, Jerry called to me.

"Drive safe," he said. "I'll see you again."

I made my way to my trusty red Corolla.

FRIDAY, I SAT WITH two young guys who visited Las Vegas for the first time. They decided on a tattoo to celebrate the loss of their virginity, which they planned for that evening. Trying not to be grossed out by their childish prattle on the evening's plans, I showed them various tattoo samples.

"Nah, I don't like any of these. Can I see yours?" One said with a smirk. This again reminded me I didn't have any visible tattoos.

"Sorry, mine are private," I pulled out another sample book. Finally, the two hormone-laden teens selected tattoos. I then convinced them that Adam would do the best job, since I was only an apprentice. I steered them both into the back room with Adam.

With them out of the way, I let out an audible sigh.

"You'll get used to that."

I looked up and found Pamela smiling at me. "Yeah, I guess."

I put away the books when an idea hit. Why couldn't I put temporary tattoos on my arms when I worked? I remembered when Adam had shown me how to apply the transfers and how they had been easy to wash off. That might solve my problem with the customers, but I wouldn't be stuck with anything permanent. I sat down and began to draw some designs. I kept my head down when the two guys loudly exited the back room, which caused Pamela to compliment their new tats on their way out. I continued to draw when the bell above the door clanked. I raised my head.

Jerry walked into the parlor and I felt myself smile. I couldn't help noticing the small wrinkle at the edges of his golden eyes.

"Anyone up for dinner?" he asked.

Adam, who now stood next to the front desk, looked at Pam and she gave a quick nod.

"Nah," Adam said. "Got to finish the books tonight."

"Yes, we'll probably be here a few more hours. You know taxes and stuff," Pam said, "Why don't you two go?"

Jerry looked at me and I noticed Pam had a faint smile on her face.

"Okay with me." Jerry said. "You want to have a quick bite?"

"Okay." I answered.

We left Pam and Adam sitting by her laptop, looking at the ledger. Somehow, I got the feeling they weren't all that interested in the books, but I shrugged it off and headed out and onto Fremont with Jerry.

It was a warm summer evening, but not too warm. I seldom allowed myself the luxury of walking along the strip. But tonight, I enjoyed the bright lights and buzz of excitement. We walked in silence for a couple of minutes and then Jerry spoke.

"What brings you to Las Vegas?" he asked.

"Oh, you know. Getting away from a small town."

"Where are you from originally?"

I felt oddly uncomfortable lying to Jerry. "I'm from Ohio. A suburb of Cleveland. What about you?" I attempted to change the subject.

"Me? I was born and raised in Vegas. Can you believe it?"

I looked up and saw his dazzling smile and deep-set eyes looking at me. I looked down. We continued to walk. I talked on about tattoos. Jerry reached out and touched me on the shoulder.

"Here we are."

A green and red canopy with the name Delmonico's covered the entrance. I stopped, ran my hands over my all black outfit with the clunky boots and was embarrassed. In the mirrored glass of the front door, I attempted to smooth down the spiked wig.

"I'm not sure I'm dressed for this place."

"Don't even worry about that." He led me through the door.

A large man stood at a lectern. He looked at a seating chart. A small gooseneck lamp illuminated his face. He looked up when we approached and then smiled.

"Hey, my friend. Table for two?" He ignored my punk rock clothing and I relaxed.

"Sure thing, George." Jerry responded.

The Maître de took two menus from under the lectern and waited for me to walk ahead of Jerry. He led us to a private booth toward the back of the restaurant, handed us the menus and left.

"I'm not out of place?" I questioned.

"Just enjoy yourself. They have some of the best pasta in Vegas. Been coming here for years." Jerry pushed his menu aside. "I'd recommend the capellini pomodoro. I usually get it with goat cheese sprinkled over it."

"Sounds fine with me. I love pasta."

George returned with a bottle of red wine and set it before us.

"Thanks, George," Jerry said. "I'll just have a glass, but the lady does not drink."
"May I just have an iced tea?"

He nodded and walked away with the bottle of wine. Minutes later he returned with a frosty glass of iced tea and red wine for Jerry.

"Can you tell Mario we'll have two of the usual?" George lowered his head and backed away.

Jerry picked up his glass of wine and held it up for a toast. I gently tapped my iced tea against his wine glass.

"To new friends," he said.

"How long have you known Adam?" I asked.

"Actually, Adam is my brother."

"Your brother? You don't look anything alike."

"My father is one of the largest contractors in Vegas. Built several of the casinos here. With big money comes excess. My dad loved living the big life. Gambling, liquor, and, of course, women. Adam's

mother was one of the dancers at The
Flamingo."

"I didn't mean to be so nosey."

"Hey. Don't worry about it. Adam and I
are fine with it. I didn't even meet Adam
until I was ten. His mother died in a car
accident when Adam was eight. There was no
one else to take care of him. My dad was
going to send him off and be done with it.
But my mom found out about Adam and
wouldn't hear of it. She brought him home
to live with us. He came from a ratty
apartment on the west side of town into our
big house."

Jerry took a sip of his wine. "At
first, I was pissed. But Adam is a special
guy and my mom always treated him like a
son. In fact, my mom never treated him any
different from me, made sure he felt like
one of the family. And Adam was always so
cool. I really enjoyed having him for a
younger brother. He's a smart guy, too.
Would you believe he got an MBA in only a
year?"

"You're kidding me."

"No. Adam is Adam. Never put on
pretenses, never wanted anything. Never
asked for anything from anyone. He started
getting tattoos in school and fell in love
with it. He finished his degree, but kept
taking art classes and apprenticed in
tattooing. Dad wasn't so happy, but mom was

proud when Adam bought his own parlor. He also invested in stocks and has done well. He and Pam are just happy living like they are. They have a nice apartment, but nothing fancy. Guess we both took after my mom and her influence rather than my dad."

When the waiter put the pasta in front of us, Jerry paused and looked at me.
"Do you mind if I say a short prayer?"

Surprised, I nodded. He reached out and took my hand in his and said grace. I found myself caught between pleasure, guilt and embarrassment. But, when he finished the prayer, I did the sign of the cross without a thought.

The pasta was delicious and I loved the addition of goat cheese to the delicate flavor of basil and garlic.

"Enough about me," Jerry said. "What about you?"

I looked into those amber eyes and my heart fluttered. I didn't want to lie, but I had no choice.

"Nothing special. My parents died in a car accident just after I graduated from high school. I got a small insurance policy, so I left the Midwest behind and moved to Vegas. I've been working in small casino. Then I met Adam and here I am. The day job pays the rent, but I really want to be an artist."

"Sorry about your parents," Jerry said and waved to George to order dessert.

"Are your parents still alive?" I asked before he could say another thing. George came over quickly and Jerry ordered a dessert.

"Yes. They are in Europe for a month. Would you believe my father completely changed his ways after Mom took in Adam? I think he saw her for the wonderful woman she is."

"That's wonderful. Are you close to your parents?" I took a bite of the tiramisu. "This is delicious."

"I hope you don't mind sharing." he said, taking a small bite.

"No problem."

"Very close," Jerry continued. "In fact, I'm working part-time at the company while I finish school."

"Finish school?"

"I finished my Bachelors early, but had just started my Masters when I enlisted. I also go to school in an accelerated program. I should be done in a few months. Then I can compete with my baby brother." Jerry laughed. "Did you go to college?"

"No," I started feeling guilty. "I was going to go, but just never did." Before he could ask another question, I added. "How about Pete? What's his story?"

"Pete? What a great guy. Adam volunteered for a halfway house during school and Pete was trying to get himself clean. Now he's part of Adam's and Pam's family. Cleaned up himself, got married and has that little boy he keeps tattooing on his arms."

We polished off our tiramisu and Jerry asked for the check. I noticed Jerry slap a wad of cash into the waiter's hand when he presented Jerry the bill.

"Let's walk back," he said. He guided me out of the booth. We left the quiet restaurant. Jerry took my hand and together we returned to the glare of neon lights. I found myself relaxed and interested in everything Jerry told me about his family and the war in Afghanistan. Even though we had walked blocks, we arrived back at the tattoo parlor in what seemed like only a few minutes. He made sure I was safely in my car and driving away before he went to his own car.

Unfortunately, I didn't even care if anyone followed me tonight. In a pleasant fog, I arrived at my apartment and nearly floated up the stairs. I dreamed about the handsome man I just shared the evening with.

FOURTEEN

New York - Five Years Ago

I STOOD at the upstairs window, hiding behind the curtains. Carlo and his entourage of criminals entered two black Lincolns and headed down the tree-lined driveway. Only after they drove off, I realized I was clenching the delicate lace. Once the cars were out of sight, I left my bedroom and went downstairs.

Over two years had passed since my thirteenth birthday celebration. At fifteen, I knew more than I ever imagined about Carlo and his criminal activities. Sure, students whispered at school, but I assumed it was only idle gossip of over-indulged teenagers. It had all come to a head the afternoon I was home for spring break.

Downstairs, Carlo yelled. I ran to the guestroom over Carlo's office, dropped to the floor and scooted under the bed to listen through the vent. There was no sound coming from below. Then Carlo began to scream at someone. This was followed by the sound of footsteps running up the stairs to the second floor. A door slammed.

I wriggled out from under the bed and hurried into the hall. I stood there and listened carefully. Nothing. Finally, I walked to my mother's room and knocked.

"Go away." My mother's voice sounded cold and distant.

I turned the knob and peeked inside. Mother sat at her dressing table pouring amber liquid from a crystal decanter into a glass. Her skin was pale, with a yellowish hue.

"Mom?"

Mother turned her head toward my voice and then quickly turned away. But even in that quick movement, the swollen cheek and red eyes were visible.

"Are you okay?"

"I'm not feeling well right now, Mandy. Can we talk later?" Kathryne's words were slow and deliberate.

I remained by the door. Mother nursed her ever-present drink. She was drinking more and more. Fights between her mother and Carlo were escalating, but this was the first time there were bruises. Now I waited, watching my mother.

A muffled gasp from my mother brought me back to the moment. My hand still rested on the doorknob.

Mother dabbed at her eyes and took another drink. She turned slowly and looked at me.

"Sorry, I am feeling under the weather. I think I'm going to bed early." Mother turned away.

I was about to leave when Mother blurted. "You know he killed your father?"

I stopped in my tracks, still facing the doors, but kept my back to Mother. "I know," I whispered and closed the door.

I went downstairs to check on Carlo's whereabouts. I was relieved to find he had left town and would be gone until tomorrow. With no one else around, I headed to his office. I slipped into the large room and went directly to his desk. Sliding open the top right drawer, I reached under and pulled off the small card was taped to the wood. I found the combination.

It took me two years to learn where he kept it. Using Carlo's affection for me, I worked my way into being his little helper. I knew Carlo was grooming me to take over his business enterprise and was more than willing to share minor secrets. He often let me help with the accounting and other financial activities. By watching carefully, I figured out where he kept the combination. I knew I would find what she wanted.

When I look at the combination, I laughed out loud, then quickly covered my mouth. The combination was my own birthday. I returned the card, making sure I put it back exactly the way I found it. Looking up to the wall opposite Carlo's desk, I stared at the impressionistic painting by Andrea Fortini. I pulled a pair of latex gloves out of my pocket and put them on. I pulled the right side of the painting toward me, which revealed the wall safe. The dial turned easily back and forth. I put in the month, day and year. Each number was followed by a barely audible click. My hands shook as I pushed down the lever and pulled the metal door toward me. In the three-foot by three-foot metal container, I found myself staring at secured bundles of brand new one hundred-dollar bills. The entire bottom two feet of the safe was jammed with cash. On the top of a shelf was a leather pouch.

I removed it from the safe and went over to Carlo's chair. The elastic strap snapped when I opened it and peered inside. I removed the entire stack of documents and placed them on the table in front of me. One by one, I turned them over, snapped a photo with my cellphone and read. Anger coursed through me and threatened to make my head explode. I wanted to scream, to cry. But I contained myself and returned the contents to the pouch and put it back in the safe. After locking the safe I turned on the computer and searched through Carlo's files. Any high schooler could figure out his system. I took out a flash drive and copied several files. Carlo's own obsessive behaviors would someday be his downfall. After I put everything away, I left the room.

All I needed now was time. Time to put my plan together. The first thing I needed to do was delay my high school graduation. Since I could easily graduate at sixteen, I needed to take additional classes and postpone others until I was eighteen.

The next semester I signed up for more electives and fewer business classes. It was obvious that Carlo was not happy when I started adding art classes to my curriculum, but he never denied me a thing. I sustained my straight A average, which appeased him and I continued to make plans to attend Harvard Business School. I also started learning the construction industry and accompanied Carlo when he went from job site to job site.
□

FIFTEEN

Current Day

THE SIDEWALK IN front of the tattoo parlor radiated heat. Outside, people struggled through the 110-degree temperatures. Those holding plastic tourist cups from Margaritaville appeared oblivious to the scorching sidewalk. From my perch on the worn gray sofa, I watched through the neon sign in the window. Inside the shop the air conditioner fought to hold its own against the hot summer. I sat in the reception area, my feet on the couch and drawing pad on my lap. I put finishing touches on my ideas for some temporary tattoos then heard the overhead bell announced a visitor.

"I know what I want." Jerry's deep voice announced. He stood just inside the door, his large frame backlit by brilliant sunshine.

"What?" Pam and Adam stood at the counter. As usual, Pam tapped away on her keyboard and Adam stood next to her, staring at the screen. Pam closed the computer.

"Yeah, what do you want?" Adam repeated.

"The idea for my tattoo," Jerry said. "I want a mean rattler on my back."

"That's cool." I added my two cents. I put down my drawing pad and lowered my feet from the sofa. Jerry came further into the shop and moved out of the blinding light. I had a better view and I coughed to regulate my beating heart.

Turning, he pointed at me, "I want you to do it." He looked over at Adam. "Sorry, man, but she's better than you."

"Me?" I said. "But I've only been doing tattoos for six months. Why don't you have Adam do it? When have you even seen my drawings?"

"Adam's shown me." Jerry said. "Your sketches are great."

"Hey, don't put yourself down," Adam added. "You're a much better artist than I am. It won't offend me."

"Do it, Nikki," Pam added. "Adam always raves about your skills. Do it."

"Are you sure?" I asked.

"I am." Jerry stared into my eyes. "Do you want to start now?"

"Whew, I've got to get a drawing put together and then do the transfer."

"Well, what are we waiting for?"

With no appointments for the rest of the afternoon, Jerry and I began the design. At closing time, we called in Pam and Adam to show them what we had done.

I held up the drawing for their approval. It measured around 12 X 18 and would cover Jerry's entire back. A menacing rattlesnake coiled and ready to strike. It bared its fangs. It was beautiful and fearful. The rattles appeared to vibrate and the eyes gleamed with anger. It prepared for its attack. Several boulders and a cactus, covered with red and yellow blossoms, dotted the background.

"Nikki, you outdid yourself," Adam whispered. Pam nodded.

Pete came into the main room from his cubicle and whistled when he saw the drawing. "Man, I should let you start doing my tats."

They all laughed, but my face felt hot.

Jerry pointed to the clock. "It's a little late today. Let's go get a bite to eat and I'll come by on Wednesday to start."

Pam opened her laptop. "You guys go ahead. I've still got work to do."

Adam moved toward Pam. "Yeah, lots of work to do. Go ahead without us."

    It was then I saw Pete step forward,
but Adam nudged him with his elbow.
    "I can't go," Pete said. "Got a client
coming in soon." He turned and went back to
his cubicle.

    And I thought Pam didn't like me.
Surprise, surprise.

SIXTEEN

New York – Two Years Ago

CARLO'S MERCEDES stopped in front of the house. I turned away from my bedroom window, slipped off my jeans and top and pulled on a one-piece bathing suit. The front door slammed just as I slipped the straps over my shoulders. After grabbing a towel from the bathroom, I ran down the stairs.

"Papa!" I yelled when Carlo entered the foyer. "Welcome home." With a towel draped over my shoulder, I reached up and kissed him on the cheek. Jorge averted his eyes, like a dutiful employee. Max, who was standing by the door to the living room, continued to look straight ahead. Carlo quickly eyed my figure, then leaned down and grabbed the towel. He pushed it toward me and turned to see Roberto standing in the hall by the dining room door, a large sandwich held halfway to his open mouth.

"What are you looking at?" Carlo said in a loud voice. Roberto turned and went back toward the kitchen. Carlo's voice softened. "Mandy, where is your robe?"

I tipped my head coyly. No longer the innocent teenager, I knew how to manipulate Carlo. My eighteen-year-old body had ripened and I knew Carlo was aware of it.

"Upstairs, Papa. I'll go get it." I turned and headed up the stairs, making sure no one could see my grin. Then I stopped midway. "Papa, I got my tickets for the trip. Thank you."

As my graduation present, Carlo had reluctantly agreed to let me attend art school in Paris for six weeks. A chaperone would accompany me at the school, but I had convinced Carlo and Kathryne to let me fly on my own, with no bodyguards. Only I knew I would never arrive in Paris.

I went into my room and picked up the soft chenille robe from the bed. I shrugged into it. Material things meant so little to me these days. The French perfumes, the designer clothes, the jewelry, the electronics. They were of no consequence. My heart and mind were filled only with hatred and revenge for the death of my father.

From the bottom drawer of my dresser, I took out one of the large envelopes taped to the underside. I pried apart the metal tabs and several drivers' licenses fell onto the carpet. I took the stack of papers and flipped through the various birth certificates I had collected over the last two years. Then I returned the items to the envelope and taped it to the drawer. An identical envelope, its contents bulging, was taped to the other half of the drawer. In that one was several thousand dollars of

American Express traveler's checks in names
matching some of the IDs.

Today, Carlo was returning from the
bank with the last of the traveler's checks
for my trip. These checks would have the
serial numbers I needed for the next part
of my plan. I returned the drawer and
stood. Mother's silver framed photograph,
taken right before father had died, sat on
the dresser. I gently tucked the photo in
among my clothing. Only those possessions
that would be expected to go with me on the
trip would be packed and most of those
would be thrown away. I turned away from
the painful memories and headed down to the
pool.

A WEEK LATER, I was ready for the next
step in my plan. The rasp of the zipper
seemed overly loud when I closed one of her
three suitcases. I stuffed a few articles
of clothing from a local thrift shop around
the cash in one of the large pieces of
luggage. I was glad the suitcase was sturdy
and rolled easily on wheels. Early that
morning, I had visited Carlo's safe and
taken two million in hundred-dollar bills
and stacked them in a suitcase. His safe
held over ten million and I arranged the
money so the missing cash was not readily
noticed. I also placed a large pouch of
diamonds in my handbag. The missing
diamonds would be easier to detect, but
Carlo was busy with a planned meeting with
the Governor and would most likely not look

for them, at least until after I had left on my trip.

One large suitcase already sat by the door, packed with my favorite clothing and accessories. I had put a flower decal on this one so as not to confuse the two. When I was done arranging the money in my second large suitcase, I placed a layer of clothing on top and zipped it up. Then I placed a lock on both, just to be sure. One last check of the carry-on ensured everything was the way I needed it. I would also carry a large handbag on my shoulder. It contained several packs of cash, travelers checks from Carlo, my various identification cards and a few other essentials. From the album on my dresser, I pulled out the only photo I had of my father, hidden between two other photographs. I put it inside a separate pouch of my handbag and called to Jorge to come get my luggage.

Most of the photographs of my father seemed to disappear after mother's marriage to Carlo. The only one I had was from a visit to a carnival before father died. I had kept it tucked in a drawer for years and now carried it along with the childish drawing of my father in a small velvet jewelry pouch. I stood in front of the mirror one last time. I wore a thin tunic over black leotards with flats.

Mother, her skin sallow, stood in the foyer with Carlo beside her.

"I think it would be wise for Max to go with you," Carlo said.

"Papa, I'll be eighteen in a month and you promised I could take this trip on my own. I'll only be gone eight weeks."

"Let us at least go to the airport with you," he pleaded.

"Papa, come on, it's just art school and if you go, you'll be late for your meeting at the Capitol. Monica will arrive next week and we'll be in school together." Even my friend, Monica, was unaware of my plan. "I want to visit the museums again and get acquainted with the art before I start the academy next week. Don't forget, this is for fun. In the fall, I start my MBA program and won't have time for any drawing. But you promised. Besides, you know you can't go through security, so why go all the way there just to say goodbye before I even get to the gate?"

Carlo sighed. "Yes, but you know we worry about you."

Mother stood stoically and kissed my cheek. A strange sadness filled mother's eyes. It was almost as if she knew she would never see me again. I hugged Carlo and gave him a quick kiss on the cheek.

"Did you put the traveler's checks in your purse? Do you have your tickets and passport?" Carlo asked.

"Papa! Stop it! I am not a little girl." He smiled and touched my hair. With that, I turned and walked through the door Jorge was holding open for me. Max was standing by the car, waiting. Having Max for a driver worried me, but there was little I could do now. I let Max load the two large suitcases and the carry-on into the trunk. He looked at me for a few seconds after hefting the large suitcase in the truck. I wondered for just a moment if he had any idea what was in it but shook it off and climbed into the back seat. I remained quiet throughout the drive, as did Max.

At the airport, Max loaded my luggage on a cart and looked down at me. "You be careful, Miss." I looked up in surprise. I couldn't remember the last time he truely spoke to me. I looked back and waved back then went into the terminal.

Once inside, I hurried to a kiosk and then glanced back to see a police officer directing Max to move the car. Good! He would have no way of watching me. I waited another five minutes, then heaved the suitcase with the decal onto the baggage check-in stand and presented my ticket.

"Do you want to check all your bags?" the agent asked.

"No, thank you. The other bag is my friend's. She'll be here soon with her ticket and she can check it. I'll take the carry-on with me." I didn't want anyone suspicious why I was not checking the other bag and that it would be leaving the airport with me.

Instead of heading toward the departure gate, I walked away, struggling with the other two pieces of luggage. Away from the ticket counter, I went into a bathroom near an exit. Once inside, I negotiated the bags into a stall. From the smaller bag, I removed a wrinkled Denim jacket, well-worn jeans, scuffed tennis shoes and a faded ball cap. I pulled out the tunic and tied it around my waist. I slipped on the jeans over my leotards, replaced the Mary Janes with the tennis shoes and tucked my hair under the baseball cap. I placed the shoes I'd been wearing into the bag and put on a pair of large of sunglasses. Just before leaving the stall, I took a tube of superglue out of my purse, rubbed it onto my fingertips and blew on them until the glue was dry. When I exited the stall, I bore little resemblance to the young woman who had entered.

With my head down, I pulled my bags back out to the curb. There was no sign of Max and the Lincoln, so I crossed the street and entered the parking garage. On the second floor of the structure an older model, non-descript Ford waited. Only a few weeks before, I'd paid cash for the car to a man from the Bronx. I pulled the key from my jean pocket, opened the trunk and lifted the suitcase inside. Two million dollars was heavy. I threw the smaller suitcase in next to the large one. A shopping bag filled with clothing picked up at thrift shops was crammed into a corner of the trunk.

From the glove box, I removed a long-term parking stub I'd retrieved when I parked the car there two weeks before. I started the car, put it in gear and drove to the exit. I handed him the stub and paid the fee with cash. I kept my head down.

With a full tank of gas, two million in cash in one suitcase, various forms of identification in the other, additional cash hidden in the trunk of the car and a bag full of perfect diamonds, I headed south. The first leg of the trip would take me over a thousand miles from the home I had known all my life. But this was only the beginning.

BY EARLY MORNING, my eyes started to droop. I pulled into a rest stop in Georgia and slept for a few hours. Along the way, I stopped at small gas stations and fast food places, always careful to pay cash and keep my face away from cameras. By the next evening, I arrived in Miami. This was my first destination. Exhausted, I stopped at an out-of-the-way motel to sleep for the night. After lugging the suitcases into the room, I opened the large suitcase to reveal pack after pack of one hundred-dollar bills. This, along with the money I had been putting in accounts over the last three years made a total of over three million dollars. I finally fell into bed and slept through the night.

The next day, I left the motel before dawn and drove to the beach. I was now prepared to complete the next step of my plan. Dressed in baggy jeans, overly large tennis shoes and a jacket with the hood pulled up, I walked to the beach. The air was humid, even at this early hour. The morning sun peeked over the horizon. I made sure no one was on the beach and chose a trashcan right off a parking lot. It was the perfect spot. I removed my purse from under the jacket and quickly shook the contents in and around the canister. My favorite scarf was already smeared with my blood from a cut on my now bandaged thumb. Medical gloves protected my thumb and ensured no fingerprints were left behind. Blood had also been dripped on a few of the traveler's checks, my wallet and the purse. I dropped the purse, wallet and a few of the travelers checks into the can and let the rest fly onto the sand. Next, I went to the bus station and put my suitcases into a locker, then drove to a deserted shopping mall and abandoned the car. Finally, I walked the mile back to the Greyhound station, pulled my suitcases out of a locker and boarded the Greyhound to Atlanta.

In Atlanta, I found a small motel and showered. I changed into jeans and a sweatshirt and continued on my trip. I returned to the bus station and purchased a one-way ticket to Mobile, Alabama.

In Mobile, I bought another one-way ticket to New Orleans and checked into a small hotel. The next morning, I bought a used car for $700, using one of my false IDs. I lied and told him I would change the registration right away. Back at the hotel, I packed up my suitcases and, before heading north, stopped at a costume shop in an industrial district. There I bought a black, spiked wig and several punk rock pieces of jewelry and clothing. After spending a night at a ratty hotel just outside the city limits, I packed up before dawn and headed out.

The used car ran well and I headed north on Highway 55 toward Jackson, Mississippi. Without stopping in Jackson, I headed West on the 20. Just after Vicksburg, I stopped on a bridge overlooking the Mississippi River. With the sun low in the west, I stood on the bank and took out Carlo's diamonds. The diamonds slipped from the pouch into the muddy Mississippi and the sun sparkled through the precious gemstones. Probably over a million dollars worth of grade A diamonds splashed into the river and sank into the mud. I snickered. I had no interest in keeping any of them. This was

all about making Carlo suffer and I knew
how much he loved his diamonds.

By the time anyone figured I was gone,
I was on my way to Las Vegas.

SEVENTEEN

Current Day

ON WEDNESDAY, I walked into the parlor early and found Pam staring at her computer as usual. When she looked up, she quickly closed the laptop.

"Jerry's waiting for you," she said, her face slightly flushed.

"Is everything okay?" I asked.

"Sure," she said. "He got here early." Going into the back, I found Jerry sitting on the edge of the table talking to Adam. He appeared slightly nervous.

"You ready?" I asked.

"Sure. Never thought I'd get this big of a tattoo, but why not. Let's get started." He stood.

Adam smiled at Jerry and walked out of the room.

"Take your shirt off and lie down on your stomach."

First, I cleaned Jerry's back with a mild astringent to numb the pain and then applied a layer of petroleum jelly over his back. With that done, I placed the transfer on his back that I prepared earlier. Once the transfer was in place, I rubbed the transfer until the drawing of the tattoo was transmitted to his skin.

"Are you okay for me to start?" I asked.

Jerry nodded. "Yep, been there."

"I'm going to start with the lighter colors first, then fill in with the darker colors. Let me know if it gets too painful or if you get tired."

I changed my latex gloves, took the sterilized tattooing needle and filled it with a light color of ink. Then I carefully began to fill in the lighter areas of the tattoo. This process made it easier to know where to put the darker ink and it was easier to ink over the light areas than the dark if you made any mistakes. As the ink began to create the snake, I found myself lost in the process. My arms tingled, but not from the vibration of the needle. I applied ink, wiped the excess away and then applied more. I touched Jerry's naked back and my groin grew moist.

I worked slowly, creating the gold and green scales of the rattlesnake. Its eyes glowed in the light of the lamp in the room. My entire body came alive with the sexuality and closeness of this act of applying the ink. Soon, the humming of the needle lulled me and I blinked my eyes several times. A part of me said to stop, but I felt a sensation like nothing I had ever experienced and I couldn't put down the needle.

I ran the needle over the design, changed needles, changed ink, wiped blood, wiped ink, still going. Again, I wanted to stop, but didn't. Jerry remained quiet.

"Hey, you two." Adam poked his head into the room. "You've been at it for two hours."

I looked up at Adam, barely seeing his face in the circle of darkness beyond the lamp. Then I looked down at Jerry. He was sound asleep. Adam came into the room and looked at Jerry's back.

"Wow," Adam said, his eyebrows arched. "That's a kicker. But, how did you do so much so fast?"

Without waiting for my answer, Adam poked Jerry. "Hey, man. How can you sleep through that?"

I lifted myself from the stool, took the magnifying glass from my face and looked down at the tattoo. The huge snake appeared ready to strike, its eyes seemed to glare at us. A drop of venom glistened from one fang.

Jerry stirred and stopped snoring. He turned his head and looked up. He yawned loudly. "What's it look like?"

"Unbelievable, man. I've never seen anything like it. I know it's not totally done, but it looks like it could jump off your back and bite the crap out of us right now. Later tonight, it's going to hurt like hell." Adam turned toward me. "You better clean up now and be sure to apply some more cream to take away the sting."

The beads at the front of the shop *rattled and a few seconds later Pam stuck her head into the room.*

"Can I see?" she asked and then came forward. "Damn! That's beautiful."

I was proud of all the attention and myself. I looked up at Jerry.

"Lie back down," I commanded. "I need to finish cleaning it and put on some more antiseptic." He obeyed and turned his face toward me.

"Shouldn't I be feeling some pain?" Jerry asked. "I actually don't feel anything except sleepy."

Both Pam and Adam looked at him. "Man, a tattoo that large should be really painful. I can't believe you were sleeping." Adam said. Pam nodded.

"Now, don't forget, it will take some time to heal and may be painful. Use the antiseptic cream and when you feel up to it, we'll finish the tattoo." I moved my seat away from him. I'd love to put the cream on his back, but that was pushing it.

Jerry sat up. He waited for several minutes and then stood. "Can't believe how tired I am. What did you do, drug me?"
Adam laughed.

My cheeks felt hot. "I'm sorry. I forgot you've gotten tattoos before. Adam always tells me to give all the necessary information."

"Hey, I'm just kidding." Jerry reached for his shirt and slipped into it. "I feel great."

EIGHTEEN

BORED, I SAT ON the sofa just inside the front door of the shop and stared into the street. Through the curves of the neon sign, a blur of people passed on their way to the Pedestrian Mall. Middle-aged tourists peered furtively into empty storefronts and women clutched their purses while they hurried past one of the many unsavory characters huddled in doorways. Groups of younger visitors ambled past, oblivious of the impact hard times had on businesses along Fremont Street just east of The Strip. Most likely, their only concern was the price of beer at Hennessey's Tavern or the tequila at Margaritaville.

Watching a fly crawl across the front window, I didn't see Jerry until he burst through the front door, causing the bell above the door to clank. He walked toward me and pulled me to my feet. His strong arms encased me. Before I could even respond, his mouth met mine. Like a spilled bowl of vanilla pudding, I was ready to puddle at his feet. Heat spread through my entire body. I stepped back and looked around. Pam giggled and a waiting customer snickered.

"Ready to finish?" he asked. I looked at him in shock.
"Finish? Are you kidding? We just did most of a large tattoo in one day. Aren't you still in pain?"

"Pain? Are you joking? I feel ready to climb Mount Whitney."

A curtain of plastic beads parted at the back of the store and Adam entered.

"I'm ready for you," he said to the young girl, then turned to Jerry. "How's it going?"

"Great," Jerry responded. "Ready to finish my tattoo."

"Man, you just had a major tattoo on Friday. Hey, let me take a look." Jerry stepped forward and lifted the back of his shirt.

"Wow," Adam said. "You don't even have any redness." He dropped his brother's shirt and walked around to face him. "Hey, bro. I know you think you're tough, but maybe you should hold off a day or two."

"Told you. I feel great. I want to get this done."

Adam waved his hand. "Go for it."

Adam and the girl left the room and I headed for a private room at the rear of the salon. Jerry followed.

"You two have fun in there," Pam called after us.

Once in the room, Jerry took off his shirt and sat on the table. I tried not to look at his muscular chest while I readied my implements.

"You need to pull your pants down below your waist," I said.

"Sorry," he stood, lowered his pants, got back on the table and lay on his stomach. I covered his butt.

"How long were you in Afghanistan?" I tried to focus on setting up my tools.

"I did two tours. That's four years."

"Was it tough?"

"Sure, saw a lot of bad shit."

"But, if you did two tours, doesn't't't that mean you signed up again?"

"Well, I actually got deployed just after 9/11. I was already in training when that happened."

"Why did you go in the first place?"

"That's a long story. Basically, I'd finished college and just wasn't ready to go into dad's business. Adam had already finished his MBA. He finished college before his older brother. You know, the smart one. I decided to enlist and see the world. Didn't think I'd be sent to Afghanistan right after basic."

"Were you upset to go to Afghanistan?"

"Na. Our whole unit was really revved up. We wanted to fight for our country. Still glad I did it. War is something you don't want, but it was my country that got attacked. That's really f---. Oops, sorry."

"Don't worry about it. You must have seen a lot of horrible things in Afghanistan. How do you remain so positive?"

"Like I said. It wasn't fun. But some guys just couldn't deal with the stuff they experienced. They ended up in the VA Hospital or worse. Others ended up on permanent disability with PTSD. I figured I could screw up my life more if I held onto the crap or I could get back in the game. Hey, I'm one of the lucky ones. I came back with my arms and legs. What in the world do I have to be pissed about?"

"Let me check your tat."

I rolled my chair to the table and studied the tattoo. I had finished about two-thirds of the snake. I pulled the magnifying glass closer and turned on the light to study my work. Even I was surprised at the vividness of the colors and the level of healing already apparent. I touched the scales on the snake and could almost feel each of the ridges. A shiver ran up my arm and through my chest. I pulled back and picked up my tools. "You ready?"

"Oh, by the way, wasn't able to apply any cream. Little difficult to reach back there." He laughed.

My face felt hot. "Sorry."

"No problem. Now let's rock and roll."

Once again, I made sure to remove any hair that had grown since Friday. Using a new razor, I shaved the entire area to be tattooed. I carefully cleaned his back with an alcohol-soaked cotton ball. Finally, I rubbed a thin coat of petroleum jelly over his back, my hands trembling from the touch of his warm skin. The outline of the tattoo had been completed during the first session. Now I just needed to fill in the colors.

I began work on the final inking of the snake, when an intense excitement and pleasure traveled through my fingers and through my body. I bit my lip and focused on the vibration of the needle in my hand. The low buzz of the needle lulled me into a state of calmness. My hand and fingers tingled from the constant hum as I ran the tool over Jerry's smooth back. I worked automatically, drawing, wiping, applying ink, replacing needles, drawing, wiping. My thoughts drifted while I worked.

A wave of heat ran through me. I tried to get my bearings. I was in the middle of the desert. Hot crystalline sand burned my naked skin. Beetles scurried past. A scorpion shook its tail at me then backed off and went between some small rocks. I raised my eyes. The noonday sun beat down upon me. Through the glare, a small sparrow flew past. It was followed by a red-tailed hawk. They appeared to collide in midair and the sparrow was carried off in the talons of the hawk. A mound of boulders provided a small amount of shade a short distance away. I squirmed forward and squeezed into the space and attempted to escape the heat of the sun. I closed my eyes to the glare.

A noise outside the door brought me back to the present. I looked down and was applying the final touches of green ink to a cactus just behind the snake. Oddly, there was no bleeding.

Adam knocked at the door. "Hey. It's been two hours."

I shook my head to clear it and found that Jerry snored. I touched him on the shoulder.

"We're done." I called to Adam. I began to put my tools away, feeling queasy.

Jerry opened his eyes. He turned his head toward me and gave a weak smile.

"Wow, am I tired. I'm ready to go home and sleep for a week. Must be from the trip to California." He sat up slowly. "How does it look?"

"You want to see?" I took a large hand mirror from a nearby table and positioned it so he could get a look at his back. His movements were slow. He turned his head to look at his reflection.

"What I can see looks great. Let me stand up and see it in the big mirror." He sat for several seconds and hesitated before getting off the table. Hit pants began to slip down further on his hips. I handed him a towel.

"You okay?" I asked.

"Sure. Like I said, I'm just really tired." He stepped up to a full-length mirror and twisted to admire his back.

"Dynamite! Best tattoo I've seen in years." His words were low and garbled.

"You sure you're okay?"

"Yeah, babe." He leaned down and kissed me lightly on the lips. My lips tingled. "Come by my home later and you can check on me." He leaned in again and lips lightly over mine.

"Sure, I can check on you to make sure you're okay."

"Can you be there about six?" he asked. "We'll put some steaks on the grill and share some iced tea." He winked and headed out the door. I walked out the door in time to see Jerry whisper to Pam while I took implements to the sterilization unit. Pam's laugh clattered like the glass shards of a wind chime.

A HOT DESERT WIND blew in from the east when I arrived at Jerry's house right on time. I was glad I remembered how to get there. I hesitated before putting my finger on the doorbell. Before I even pushed the bell, the door opened. There he was, standing before me.

"Hi," I stammered.

"I thought you would never get here," he said, pulling me inside the house and kissing me.

"It's just six now," I said. "How are you feeling?"

"I feel great. You ready to look at your finished product?"

"Of course. I've been waiting for it all day."

Jerry's shirt was already unbuttoned. He pulled it off and threw it on the sofa. He turned around slowly.

"I can't see the whole thing," I said.

He winked and unbuckled his khakis and pulled them down just below his waistline to reveal his entire back. I could see the muscles of his buttocks tighten.

"Well?"

I stared at his back. The snake appeared so real. For a moment, I was back in the desert. I shook my head to clear it. "Not bad, if I say so myself."

He pulled his pants back up, buckled his belt and turned around. "Well, I'm happy with it." He walked out of the room and came back with two large ice teas.

"You ready to eat?" he asked.

"Sure."

"I'll get the BBQ started. "Come on." He led me out the patio doors. He turned on the propane and the flame roared to life. I stood at the door and stared into the desert. The sun was just beginning to set and a pink tinge touched the still-blue sky. From his backyard, I looked out at sand, cactus and hills. Something was familiar. A small bird passed by. Already a few stars peeked through the night. The temperature was still in the nineties and scorching heat radiated from the dry sand.

"We'll let the grill warm up and slap on the steaks. Come on. It's cooler inside."

I sat on the leather sofa and sipped my tea. Jerry hit a button on the stereo and Michael Buble's voice filled the room. He came over and sat next to me.

"Well, Nikki. Whatever made you get into tattooing?" He leaned back.

"Uh, I just love drawing. It just kinda happened." I avoided the question. How could I say anything about my dream of being an artist? I lowered my head. Jerry reached over, lifted my chin and studied my face. Without saying a word, he leaned forward and kissed me again.

"Beautiful," he whispered. My breath came faster. I desperately wanted to pull off my wig and throw it on the floor. I longed to reveal myself completely to him but stopped. I felt like such a prude. I wanted this man, but, to me, sex and marriage went together. Maybe it was just my Catholic upbringing, but I just didn't feel comfortable in this situation. Then I thought about what God would say about stealing Carlo's money, and I sat up abruptly. I was such a phony. A fake. A liar.

What was I doing? I knew nothing about sex. Other than a few stolen kisses, I was a virgin. With all the Spring Break trips with my rowdy friends, I had been too busy building my new life to have a relationship. I was nothing but lies and here I was about to expose it all. Was it my fear of relationships after watching Carlo and my mother or was it my Catholic school training? My body tensed. Jerry sat back.

"Are you okay?" He had a puzzled expression on his face.

"I, I'm sorry. I've never done this before." I started to cry.

"You haven't?"

Ashamed, tears spilled from my eyes.

He reached for me and pulled me into his arms. He wiped the tears from my cheeks. "Hey, stop. We can take our time."

Was this man for real? I lifted my face to kiss him, but he placed his fingers over my *lips*.

"*Shush*," he murmured. "I want it to be very special for you. We can wait."

"I should leave," I said, mortified at my own stupidity and shame.

Jerry rose from the couch and took a deep breath. "No. You stay right here. I said I wanted you to come over. Let's have those steaks and enjoy ourselves."

I stared at him. I didn't believe I heard him right. He began preparing our dinner. We ate steaks, cooked to perfection, a fresh green salad and we both drank iced tea. When we finished dinner, we sat and listened to music.

"I want you to trust me. You're safe with me."

He reached up and touched my hair. The grin on his face puzzled me, but I remained quiet.

"Wow, now I'm really tired." He sat back and put his right arm around me and pulled me to his chest. In a few minutes, he fell asleep. I lay in the darkness thinking what I should do next. Should I run? Thoughts tumbled around in my mind until I could no longer keep my eyes open.
□

NINETEEN

I OPENED MY EYES and peered into the darkness. I expected to find Jerry next to me on the couch and reached for him. He wasn't there. Silence filled the room. I listened, but there was nothing.

"Jerry?" I sat up. A warm breeze blew in through the open sliding glass door. "Jerry?" I put my feet on the floor and slid on my sandals. At the patio door, I peered into the blackness and called his name. No answer. A hot desert wind blew into the room. I reached out and slid the door shut. I turned back to the living room, a noise from behind startled me. I turned expecting to see Jerry at the patio door. Outside, a large rattlesnake was coiled just inches away on the outside of the glass. It struck at the glass, and I screamed.

Again, I yelled his name. My mind raced. Was he still outside? Maybe he was upstairs. I ran up the steps, sure he had gone to his bedroom. Both the bedroom and bathroom were empty. The open door! What if he had gone outside to get fresh air? What if he was bitten and needed my help? I ran to the phone and called 911.

"911. How can I help you?"

"I think Jerry's outside," I yelled into the phone. "There's a snake out there. He might have been bitten."

"Slow down, miss," the male voice directed. "Tell me where you are."

I gave the operator Jerry's address.

"I think he went outside, but he's not answering and there's a rattlesnake on the porch."

"Okay," the operator responded. "Are you safe?"

"Yes."
"Give me your name."

I stopped and gaped at the phone in my hand. What was I doing?

"Nikki," I said. "Nikki."

"Okay, Nikki. The ambulance and police are on their way. Please stay on the phone?"

"I need to call Adam," I said. "Adam is Jerry's brother."

"Remain on the line until the police arrive."

"But I need to call Adam," I pleaded.

"If you're sure you're okay."

"Yes," I responded and broke the connection.

I dialed Adam's cell phone. Pam answered.

"Pam, it's Nikki. Can you and Adam come over? I think Jerry's in trouble." I gave her a quick explanation and hung up.

I walked back and forth. What was I going to do? Would the police see I had a fake ID? Would I be found out? I wanted to run, but I knew I couldn't leave. The 911 operator had my cell phone number. I had to stay or I'd be a suspect for sure.

Within ten minutes two police officers arrived. Adam and Pam followed them in. I explained everything to the policemen and Adam quickly took over. Adam told them Jerry had just returned from Afghanistan and may be experiencing PTSD. That seemed to take the focus off me. Pam guided me to the kitchen.

The police searched and the snake was nowhere to be found. They called in animal control anyway. An officer advised me they often eradicated snakes from the area and not to worry. The police checked the area immediately behind Jerry's home in case he had been bitten and wandered away. The local hospitals were also notified. I provided contact information and waited until everyone was gone. In the light of dawn, Adam, Pam and I locked up.

"I'm worried about you," Pam said, a concerned look on her face.

"I'll be okay. But, what about Jerry? Shouldn't we wait here in case he calls home or they find him?"

"Let's get you taken care of first, "Adam said. "The police will get in touch with me."

"Shouldn't we go out and search?"

"No. It's not safe. The police are bringing in a Search and Rescue Team. We will do better to stay out of their way and wait." Adam dug car keys out of his pocket. "Where's your car?"

"In Jerry's guest spot." I said.

"Leave it there. You're coming with us."

Adam took me by the elbow and led me to a black Lexus SUV I had not seen before. Pam got into the back with me and put an arm around me.

"Jerry will be fine," she said. Adam looked back and nodded. He started the car and headed away from Jerry's.

Exhausted, I closed my eyes as we traveled through the city. When the car stopped, I looked up expecting to see Adam and Pam's apartment. Instead, Adam was punching in a code at a gate. I sat up. The gates slid open and we traveled along a long driveway to a Frank Lloyd Wright style home. The house was all angles and straight lines. Dark wood framed large windows with brushed steel frames. This didn't look like Adam's apartment building. At the front entrance, Adam stopped the car and jumped out. He opened the door for Pam and me.

"Where are we?" I asked.

"This is our house," Pam said.

"Your house?" I asked.

"Yes," Adam added. "We just bought it. We were going to surprise you and Jerry with dinner. Come on. We have something to show you."

He unlocked the door and entered the foyer. He flipped a switch and a large chandelier of glass and chrome threw shards of light around the entrance, illuminating a large staircase leading up to a second story.

"This is yours?" I asked.

"Hey, didn't Jerry tell you that we aren't just the owners of a lowly tattoo parlor? We also have investments." I stared at Adam and Pam. Adam lowered his head, shyly.

"Yes, it seems my guy here is somewhat of an investment genius." Pam said.

"Speak for yourself," Adam said. "We have something to show you. Come."

I followed them into a large office void of any furniture except for a large brushed metal and glass desk and a high-back leather office chair. A late model Macintosh sat in the center of a desk. Pam went over and turned it on. She sat in front of the computer, hit several keys and waited.

"Please don't be scared, Nikki. Just don't forget we're your friends." She turned the computer toward me and sat back. I looked at the screen and took a quick breath. On the screen was a story about Amanda Nicole Rinaldi. The article described the search for her whereabouts and offered a reward for Amanda or her kidnappers. My picture filled the screen. I pulled back.

"I don't understand." I said. "Who is this?"

Adam stepped up to Pam, who now stood beside the desk.

"Pam found this a couple of months ago," Adam said. "We know."

I inched away, looking for a way to escape. Adam reached out his hands.

"Amanda, or Nikki if you like. We have no interest in any reward money." He waved his arm. "Does it look like we need it?"

"Hey, I know I was a bitch in the beginning," Pam said. "But Jerry is already falling for you."

"What?" My entire façade fell away. "Does he know?" I caught myself. "I mean, did you tell him?"

Pam pulled me to her. "Nikki, it's okay. You're safe. You're part of our family."

The years of hate welled up inside me. I sobbed. Pam offered me some water and a tissue. I cried until I ran out of tears. When I could cry no more, I looked up at them. "What about Jerry?"

"Jerry can take care of himself," Adam said. "But I have to ask. Do you think this has anything to do with your stepfather?"

"I don't think so," I said. "There really was a large rattlesnake. I think Jerry went outside. No one else was around."

"Okay. Don't worry. We'll find him. But I think you should stay here until we do."

The next night, both Adam and Pam accompanied me to my apartment. I retrieved a few items from the secret storage area in

the closet and grabbed some clothes. When
we arrived back at their new home, I moved
into a spare bedroom.
￮

TWENTY

I HAD JUST COMPLETED a palm tree on a guy's leg when Adam walked into the room and tapped me on the shoulder. His eyebrows knitted together in concentration. He lifted his finger to his lips before I could say anything. I cleaned up the tattoo, gave the usual instructions and ushered the guy out the door.

With the client gone, I asked. "What?"

Pam walked quickly to the door, locked it and turned over the open sign.

"They found Jerry," Adam said.

"Found him? Where?" I asked.

"Is he okay? Where has he been for the last three days?" Pam said.

"He was about three miles from his home, nude and dehydrated. He's okay. He's at Spring Valley Hospital. Come on. Let's go."

"Nude? That doesn't make sense." I quickly pulled off my apron and went into the main lobby.

Adam handed the keys to Pete. "Take care of things. Okay?"

Pete watched when we all left through the back door. We jumped into Adam's old truck and headed to the hospital. Adam got Jerry's room number and, together, we went upstairs. We found Jerry's room and Adam went in.

Pam followed Adam in. I hung back in the hall. Jerry lay on the bed, hooked to monitors, his skin burned. Jerry hugged his brother and sister-in-law. Then Jerry looked toward the door. Pam turned away from the bed, came out of the room, grabbed my arm and pulled me inside.

"Come on, you nut. He's waiting for you."

I approached the bed slowly. Jerry reached out the hand not connected to an IV and pulled me toward him.

"Hey, you. How are you?" he said hoarsely.

"I'm sorry," I said.

"Sorry for what?"

"For what happened to you. What did happen to you?"

"Yeah," added Adam. "What happened to you?"

Jerry looked at us, still holding my hand.
"You know," he said. "I have no damned idea. I fell asleep with this lovely lady

in my arms. Next thing I knew I was out in the desert, stark naked."

Pam raised her eyebrows and smiled.

"Nothing happened," Jerry said.

"Then you don't know about the snake?" Adam asked.

"Snake? What snake?"

"Amanda, I mean Nikki, saw this big-assed rattler outside your window when you disappeared." I jumped when Adam said my name, but Jerry never even flinched. "We had animal control and police looking for a rattler, but never found. We all thought you'd been bitten."

Pam laughed. "Maybe your snake came alive," she said.

"Yeah, sure," Jerry scoffed.

The conversation about the snake was quickly forgotten when a doctor came to the door and knocked.

"Hey, Jerry. How are you feeling?"

"Much better, doc. When can I go home?"

"I can sign you out today. The only after effect is a bad sunburn. Just take it easy for the next couple of days and come back and follow up with your primary care physician in a week or so."

After the doctor signed the discharge forms, the nurse removed the IV and helped Jerry into the bathroom. Adam handed him the clothes he had brought and soon we were on our way back to Adam and Pam's new house.

Jerry congratulated them on their new house and they showed him to a room they had set up for him. Jerry settled into bed and I went up to the guest room and started to pack. There was a noise behind me and I turned to see Jerry standing in the doorway. Pam stood next to him, her hands on her hips.

"What do you think you are doing?" he asked.

"It's time for me to go home," I responded.

"Forget that right now. Come downstairs. We all need to talk."

I followed them to the dining room. Adam sat at the table, a frosty mug of beer in front of him. Jerry motioned me to take a seat and then sat down next to me. He winced when he lowered himself into the chair.

"What's going on?" I asked.

"Well," Jerry began. "I think it is time you come clean."

"I'm s-sorry," I lowered my eyes. "I didn't mean to lie to you."

"Nikki, do you mind if I call you Amanda?" Jerry asked.

I looked away.

"I knew there was something wrong the first time we went out. You should know that Pam's brother is an FBI agent and she was able to do some research. She can track a particular flea on a particular dog. So," he said, "she got some information on missing redheads and put two and two together."

I looked at Pam. She smiled and shrugged. "Sorry."

"Either way," Jerry continued. "It doesn't matter. I care about you. Nikki, Amanda, whoever you are.

My mouth opened and Pam laughed.

"Close your mouth," she commanded. "You didn't fool us for a minute. Why do you think I didn't like you at first? I knew you were hiding something. You're too damn sweet to be a punk rocker chick."

They all laughed and finally I found myself laughing too. Then Jerry *got serious*.

"*Did* you hear what I said?" Jerry said.

"Yes," I lowered my eyes.

"Well?" Jerry said.

"I care about you, too."

Adam and Pam sighed together. "Ahhhh."

"Now," Jerry said. "Can I see you without all that crap on your face and that awful wig?"

At that moment, I was secure. Something I had not felt for a very long time.

"I think you should stay here for a while," Pam said. "If I could figure you out that easy, others might also."

Adam and Jerry agreed.

"It's not safe out there," Jerry insisted.

"I'll stay tonight, at least."

TWENTY-ONE

THE SMELL OF FRESH-brewed coffee filled the air when I walked into the kitchen. Even with the sterile atmosphere of the black granite, lacquered cabinets and brushed steel appliances, the room felt warm and inviting. I poured coffee in a tall mug and topped it off with non-dairy creamer. I turned and noticed Adam sitting at the far corner of the breakfast table, his nose buried in the Wall Street Journal.

"Good morning." I said.

He grunted, not bothering to look up. Must be an interesting article. I sat down on the opposite side of the table, my back to the door and checked out the room. It was almost hospital-like in appearance except for all the black. A movement caused me to look up and I noticed Pam outside in a garden room attached to the kitchen. The room was filled with flowers and plants. With her hair slicked back on her skull and devoid of the usual pink tints, she finished trimming the herbs and carefully putting them into a small basket hanging over her arm. She looked up and waved her small sheers, a smile on her face. Pamela put the gardening implements away on a pegboard and entered the kitchen, still carrying her basket of rosemary, basil, parsley and other herbs. I peeked in at the assortment of basil, sage, rosemary and took a deep breath.
"Hungry?" Pam said.

"Sure," I answered.

"I was thinking of making an omelet with mushrooms and these fresh herbs. Then you can take breakfast up to Jerry." She stopped halfway to the stove and put her basket on the gleaming counter.

"My God, Jerry, you look like a damn snake shedding his skin," Pam said.

"Thanks."

Jerry leaned against the doorframe. He was dressed in blue jeans, a khaki shirt and work boots. His face was red and peeling.

Adam put down his paper. "Where the hell are you going?"

"Can't sit around here all day with all of you treating me like a baby. I've got work to do."

"You sure you feel up to it?" I asked. Jerry grinned. His burnt lips cracked.

"Ouch! Yes, I'm fine. By the way, did you get that call from my friend from the Mirage? The guy who works with the tigers?"

"Yes, I already finished his drawing." I said.

Pam stopped clattering pots and pans.

"Better be careful," she laughed. "You might turn him into a tiger."

All of us turned and stared at her.

"Just kidding. But it was strange you see a snake the night after you finished the snake tattoo on Jer." She turned back to her cooking and began chopping herbs. I looked at Jerry and he winked.

"Don't worry about Pam. She thinks she has ESP."

"Stop, Jerry. You know I've had some weird experiences. Women are just more sensitive than men." Pam said.

The kitchen filled with the aroma of mushrooms simmering in butter. I thought about the strange things that happened to me over the years, but everyone already thought I had enough problems without bringing up the past.

"Can I help?" I offered.

"Sure. You can toast the English muffins and pour the juice." Pam began to beat eggs in a metal bowl. "Jerry, set the table. If you're feeling so good you can go to work, get started."

We ate fluffy omelets with fresh herbs, mushrooms and Brie and drank coffee. When done, I started clearing the table and Jerry helped.

"I'm moving back to my house," Jerry announced.

"Why? You should stay for a few more days and make sure you are fully hydrated. And what about your skin?" Pam sounded more like a nurse than a sister-in-law.

I said nothing.

"Listen, you know I like my space. Thank you for all your support. I love your new home, but I enjoy my own freedom."

"I should go home too," I said.

"Why would you want to go back to that apartment? And what about your stepfather? What if he knows you're in Vegas?" Pam sounded stressed.

"Look, I agree with Jerry. It's so nice of you and Adam to share your home, but everyone needs his or her own space. And if Carlo has found me, he would already know I work at the parlor and would have come for me. Whatever happened with Jerry probably had nothing to do with Carlo."

Pam sighed. Adam put dishes into the dishwasher.

"It's okay. But for both of you, you should know that you're always welcome here if you need a place to rest, hide out, or anything else. Let's get ready for work." Pam wiped her hands on a dishtowel.

With that, we went to our rooms to get ready and headed out the door.

THOUGH I DREAMED of being a painter, I now sat in a cubicle of the shop putting the finishing touches on a drawing of a white tiger from the Siegfried and Roy's tiger show.

"Nikki," Adam called, "Walter's here. Are you ready?"

I stuck my head out and waved at Walter.

"Sure, come on back. Just finished."

Walter was a thin man with hollow cheekbones and a head of white hair, which he wore combed back. He reminded me more of a lion than a tiger with his gaunt frame and dark brown eyes. When he looked at the drawing, he applauded and demanded that we start the next day. I worked on the transfer that evening, avoiding Jerry.

IN THE MORNING, I set up my tattooing table and was ready when the trainer walked in. He quickly took off his shirt and jumped on the table. I shaved his back thoroughly with a Bic safety razor, dried the skin and applied Speed Stick to the dry area on his back. I then pressed on the transfer. Once the tattoo transferred, I took a clean paper towel and wiped off the excess deodorant. Then I rubbed a thin layer of Vaseline across his entire back.

"Okay," I instructed. "Ready? I'll be drawing the outline of the tiger first. When that's done, I'll then ink in the darker colors. We'll finish by adding the lighter colors as we go. Of course, this entire process will be painful and we won't be able to finish it in one day."

"Right," he murmured.

"Just so you know, once the outline is completed, if you're tired or in pain, we can stop. We can continue when the swelling and redness goes down."

"Yeah, right."

I turned on the needle and began. Slowly, I traced the outline of the transfer. I used small strokes, filling in areas where necessary. I stopped every few minutes to add more ink to the needle or to wipe away excess ink and blood. As I worked, my mind began to wander. A snake crawled on the dessert floor, moving away from me. I chased after it, but it was faster and then it was gone. Without warning, I floated from the desert to the jungle. Lying on a bed of crisp, green fronds, a large white tiger with sparkling blue eyes stared at me and roared. Unafraid, I reached out my hand and the giant feline nuzzled my palm. I knelt and put my arms around the tiger's neck. I rubbed my hand against the coarse white and black fur. He purred with contently.

"Nikki," Adam's voice broke through the fog.

"What?" I jumped, almost dropping the needle. I looked down. The trainer snored.

"You've been at that for three hours." Adam stood at the door. I looked at the tattoo. The image of a ferocious white tiger covered his back, one paw lifted. Only the shine in the eyes needed to be completed.

"Wow," I said. "I didn't even know that much time had passed."

I nudged the trainer and he snorted awake. "We done?" he asked.

"Almost. How are you feeling?" I asked, concerned.

"Great," he responded. He sat up quickly. "Can I see it?"

When I turned toward Adam his eyebrows arched.

The trainer craned to see the tattoo on his back and then turned to me.

"Can't you just finish it now? You're almost done."

"It's getting late," I said and got up from my stool. "Why don't you see how you're doing tonight? If you're feeling good tomorrow, then we can finish. But I really doubt it. You will probably experience a lot of pain."

"No way," he said. "I want it done today."

"Walter, we don't usually do that size of a tattoo in one day." Adam looked at me, a look of chastisement on his face. "But since you only need to have the eyes done, go ahead. Then we can see how you feel and come back next week for any touch ups." He walked away from the cubicle.

It took about five minutes to finish. I handed Walter a tube of antiseptic cream and helped him into his shirt. After giving him some after-care instructions, I escorted him to the front desk.

Adam stood next to Pam. She worked on her computer, researching the latest trends in the stock market. Walter handed a wad of cash to Pam and left the shop.

"Amanda, I mean Nikki, you certainly have a way with tattooing. There's no one who can do that large of a tattoo in one sitting and cause no pain. Wow!" Adam said. "You really are one of the best I've seen, but you need to be careful about trying to do too much at one time. The last thing we need is problems because someone gets hurt."

"I'm sorry, Adam. The truth is, time just got away from me. I had no idea I was in there so long."

TWENTY-TWO

TODAY JERRY AND I ate lunch at Bellagio. I felt more comfortable and loved spending time with him. I left the punk rock outfit in the closet, put on the blond wig and became Robin. I waited in front of my building until Jerry drove up. Once out of the car, he whistled. He opened the car door with a sweeping gesture. "I love this new you."

I touched the blond wig on my head. "I figured this outfit was a little more conservative for lunch at Bellagio."

After turning the car over to the valet, we walked into the lobby. I looked up and stared in awe at the glass sculpture on the ceiling.

"Wow." I kept walking and stumbled right into an older woman pulling her suitcase. She grabbed at me to steady herself and accidentally broke the chain attached to the small pouch that held my father's photograph and drawing. The little bag fell to the floor.

"I'm so sorry." I helped her pick up the suitcase.

Jerry came up behind me and picked up my necklace. When the woman walked away, he took my hand and dropped the chain and pouch into it. "What is this?"

"I keep a photo of my father in it. I've had it since he died." I changed the subject and pointed up to the ceiling. "Who is the artist?"

"That sculpture is by the Chihuly. Do you like it?"

"I love it. I always wanted to be an artist," I said wistfully.

"You are," he led me through the casino. "You're an incredible artist."

"Before we try the buffet, I want to stop at a shop." He led me past the restaurant and toward the high-end stores. At Tiffany's he stopped and pulled me inside.

"What are you doing?"

The salesperson approached and asked if she could help.

"Yes," he said. "Do you have any lockets?"

"Of course, we do." She led us to a nearby counter. "We have several very nice pieces in both gold and silver."

"No," I said. "You don't have to do this. I'll just get mine fixed."

"Give me your necklace." He held out his hand.

"Please you don't have to." But I handed the chain to him.

"Can you fix this?"

The clerk checked it out and handed it back to Jerry. "Sir, this is not silver. Seems it is silver plated."

I took the chain from his hand. "That's okay. I'll just buy a new one." I turned away.

"Wait," Jerry said. "Look."

I looked where he pointed. A beautiful large, gold locket with a 24-inch rope chain hung on a velvet display. A half-carat diamond was surrounded by a ring of roses.

"We'll take that one."

"No, Jerry. You can't."

"Of course, I can."

Before I could protest further, the salesperson removed the necklace and Jerry placed it around my neck. Then he paid for it and directed me out the door.

"Now I want you to see the sculptures by Richard MacDonald." He again took my

hand and we walked past blinking slot
machines in the dim environment.

We entered the gallery, which was also
the entrance to a Circe du Soliel theater.
I left Jerry watching a video of the artist
doing his work and roamed from figure to
figure. Drawn to a life-size bronze of a
prima ballerina, I reached out to touch
her. A tear slid down my cheek as I thought
of the many things I gave up for my revenge
on Carlo.

"Hey, look at this one," Jerry said
behind me.

I turned quickly and staggered.

"You okay?"

"Sorry. Guess I was too focused on the
art."

He led me to a shelf filled with
statues each about eighteen to twenty
inches tall. "Aren't they beautiful?"

I looked at the bronze statuettes. A
smaller version of the dancer I had touched
stood before me. I moved closer.

Jerry's voice sounded far away. I
stroked the tips of her outstretched
fingers. They felt warm to the touch.

I savored the beauty of the sculpture
and then felt Jerry's hand on my shoulder.
I turned.

As we walked away, I said, "You know,
you didn't have to buy me anything."
"I wanted to. Besides, I wanted to ask
you something." He stepped close to me and
took my hands. He drew in his breath. "I
would like you to go away with me this
weekend. Will you? No expectations, no
strings."

I felt the warmth of his hand covering
mine, looked into his eyes and nodded.

"Let's eat," he said.

After gorging ourselves at the buffet,
I pulled out the pouch and showed Jerry the
contents.

"I'm sorry," he said. "I didn't know
the pouch had special meaning."

"It doesn't. Just the contents.
Actually, the locket is beautiful and much
more fitting for my father's memory." While
we sipped at coffee and tried one more
dessert, I took the photo and folded three
by five drawing from my pocket and
carefully placed them in the locket. Jerry
then placed the necklace back around my
neck and kissed me on the cheek.

Then I told him about the night my
father died.

TWENTY-THREE

"I PACKED MY HIKING clothes like you asked," I told Jerry. "But you still haven't told me where we're going."

Jerry stood holding the door open for me next to his Ford SUV. "All I'm going to say is we are going to my favorite place in Arizona. So just sit back and enjoy."

"Okay, I'm game. Do you mind if I put on some classical music?"

"Classical? I never would have expected you for that type of music."

"Actually, I have very eclectic tastes. One of my favorite CDs is Ferranti and Teicher's movie themes. I'd rather listen to classical music than modern and I also enjoy the new country." I pulled a few CDs from my bag and loaded the player. The seat tilted back easily and I closed my eyes. My heart thumped in my chest, slowly and comfortably. My thoughts strayed to my father and the early days. I breathed in deeply as strains of Mozart filled the car. All was good in my life. For the first time.

JERRY REACHED OVER and touched me. "Hey sleepy head, we're almost there."

I stretched and peered through the window. We passed forests of pine. "What time is it?"

"You've been asleep for a couple of hours," Jerry said.

"I was dreaming," I said. "Dreaming of good things." I stared out the window as Jerry slowed and started into a curve. Before me lay a pine-filled canyon. We started down a winding road.

"We're now going to go through Oak Creek Canyon. Keep an eye on the right and you'll see the creek." Jerry explained. "Next stop, Sedona."

"Sedona? Never been there." I remained quiet for several miles. I watched the trees change from spruce to hardwood. The car moved through the curves along the canyon. As we traveled around a bend, I gasped at the red rocks that came into my view.

Jerry pointed out the window. "That's Elephant Rock up ahead," he explained.

"It's gorgeous," I sat straighter to get a better view. Jerry slowed the car and we drove through the main street of Sedona. Camera-toting tourists lined the streets. Jerry pointed out other rock formations. Snoopy, Lucy, Ship Rock. Then we went around a bend and traveled past numerous homes and shops.

We entered the Enchantment Resort, stopping once to allow a deer and her fawn to cross in front of us and then pulled into a parking space. Jerry checked us in, while I stood back, somewhat embarrassed. When we walked back to our car, the sun was just setting. Light hit the rock walls in front of us, creating spectacular shadows. Various shades of reds, oranges and yellows lit the cliffs. I squeezed Jerry's arm.

"Why don't we put our stuff away and then have dinner. We have reservations at seven."

In the waning light, we walked to a building of four rooms. Jerry walked to the first unit, opened the door and stepped back, handing me the key. I looked at him, confused.

"I got us separate rooms," he said.

"Oh," I muttered.

"I'll come get you in what? Half an hour?"

"Okay," Relieved. I wanted to have sex but didn't think I was ready. I entered the room and unpacked my clothing. After showering, I stood in front of the mirror and decided not to put on the blond wig. I pulled my shoulder-length hair up into a bun, put on my makeup and a black dress and heels. Nervously, I waited at the door. Finally, Jerry knocked and I pulled the door open.

"My God, you are absolutely beautiful."

"Thank you," the felt heat rise in my face.

Jerry put his hands on my shoulders. He pulled me close and brushed his lips against mine. I shivered.

He stepped back and took a deep breath. "Let's go to dinner before I change my mind."

He made a quick call and a few minutes later a golf cart pulled up and the driver honked. We climbed aboard for the short ride to the restaurant.

We sat on a patio facing east. We watched as the sun set in the west, the moon rose above the mountains and stars filled the sky. Dinner consisted of Medallions of Filet and *Duck Confit, a goat cheese risotto and a crisp green salad. For dessert, we both had coffee (mine decaf) and a shared Crème Brule. When dinner was over, we again boarded a resort cart and returned to our suite.*

In the moonlight, Jerry walked me to my room. He kissed me gently.

"Is seven-thirty okay with you for a hike?"

"I'll be ready."

TODAY I TIED A scarf around my red
hair. Then I put on jeans, a hooded
sweatshirt and tennis shoes. I was waiting
at the door when Jerry knocked lightly.

"Ready?"

I giggled and melted into his arms.
"I'm having so much fun."

Jerry pulled out a camera. "Let's take
some photos today. You're going to love the
views."

For the next few hours, we hiked Little
Horse and Bell Rock Trails. Finally, we
arrived at the Chapel of the Holy Cross. A
pleasant tightness spread across my chest
as we walked together into the small
church. We walked through the vestibule to
the first bench in the nave. We faced the
altar and gazed through a window showing
the spectacular views of Sedona. Jerry
stood and knelt at the altar. I was
pleasantly surprised and moved to be next
to him. We both remained quiet.

Dear Lord: Thank you so much for
bringing Jerry into my life and forgive me
for all that I have done. Help me find a
way to make it right. Also, please help me
find a way to save my mother from the
clutches of Carlo.

A feeling of warmth began on my chest.
I swore the locket heated up. Jerry

whispered "Amen." I ignored the feeling, made the sign of the cross and stood.

☐

TWENTY-FOUR

BACK IN VEGAS, Jerry handed the keys to
the valet outside the Paris Hotel and
Casino and ran around to my side of the
car. He opened the door and reached for me.
He squeezed my hand and together we walked
through the hotel lobby. Today, I was in
the Robin outfit, blond wig and
conservative clothing. We wove our way
through the casino toward Gordon Ramsay's.
We bypassed high-dollar slots and blackjack
tables.

The restaurant entrance was just ahead,
when I glanced into the Salon des Table.
The emblem on the back of a black leather
jacket caught my attention. I stopped. A
man sat at a poker table with his back to
me. That jacket. I knew that jacket. A
black Cadillac surrounded by flames
emblazoned the back. The man's hair hung in
greasy curls down his neck. He turned his
head slightly to make a bed and I saw the
gold cross, with a large diamond embedded
in the center, hanging from his right ear.
I dropped Jerry's hand and took a step
back. I began to shake. It was Roberto.
Carlo's Roberto. The killer.

"What's wrong?" Jerry started, but I
pulled him away from the restaurant and
toward Le Boulevard.

"What is it?" Jerry asked.

"That's Roberto," I whispered, my voice breaking. "He murdered the Senator."

"Where? What are you talking about?" he asked. He peered around the corner of Le Cafe Ile St. Louis. I pointed to the table where Roberto sat in profile.

"Yes, that's him. I recognize his jacket." My voice was a screech. A few people turned to look at us.

"Yes, he did it. I'll never forget that jacket. He had it custom made." My knees buckled. Jerry held me up, then gently directed me in another direction.

"Why would he be here?" He asked.

"He found me. He's here to kill me." Words spilled out in a hoarse whisper as I told him more about Roberto and the things I had discovered.

"Stop," Jerry said. "We don't know he's here for you."

Jerry pulled me away from where I was watching Roberto and into the café and sat me where my back was to the casino, but he could clearly see the entrance to the poker area. He took out his cellphone and called Adam. "Hey, bro. It's me." he explained. "Nikki and I are down at the Paris. Nikki has spotted one of Carlo's men." He hesitated. "We'll wait for you in the first café on Le Boulevard. Yes, St. Louis."

JERRY AND I SAT in the café, waiting.
Jerry watched the exit of the poker area to
ensure Roberto was still there. I held onto
a latte, trying to keep my shaking hands
from spilling coffee all over the table.
Twenty minutes later, Adam walked into the
café alone. He turned, spotted us and came
over.

Adam sat down next to Jerry. "Bring me
up to date."

Jerry described Roberto and told Adam
where he was sitting. They confirmed he was
still in the same place.

Quietly, I told them about my suspicion
that Roberto had killed Senator Gomes due
to his opposition to Carlo's union
activities. I told them how it had been
reported as an accident. However,
Hortencia, my old nanny, and I had
overheard things that made us believe
differently. Roberto was involved in other
deaths. But I had no evidence. When I
finished, I looked at both men. "Where's
Pam?"

"Getting ready," Adam said.

"For what?" Jerry asked.

"It's time we put an end to Carlo's
control over Nikki," Adam said and turned
to me. "Pam and I came up with an idea, but
we'll all have to take a part."

I stared at Adam, confused. Before he could even explain further, he pointed out the café window. "There's Pam now."

I turned in my chair, making sure I stayed out of view and was shocked when I finally recognized Pam making her way through the casino toward the Salon des Tables. She was wearing a short black skirt, with a strapless gold top. Her heels were at least five inches high. Gone were the short locks, usually tipped with pink. Instead, she wore a long red wig. I cringed when I saw the wig, like my own red hair. Though Pam seldom wore makeup, today her eyes were enhanced with mascara, eyeliner and shadow. On her lips, she wore a deep red. I panicked and stood up. "You have to stop her."

Adam reached up and gently pulled me back into the seat. "Relax."

I sat down, shaking even more than before. Jerry stepped closer and put his arm around my waist. "Take a breath."

Adam reached into his pocket and pulled out a key. "Jerry, why don't you guys head back to our house? Wait there for us."

Jerry took the keys. "Do you know what you're doing?"

"Yep. Go ahead and get her home safe. I'll be there soon."

Before I could protest any more, Adam left the café. Jerry directed me to head through Le Boulevard to the self-parking area, while he went to the lobby to collect his car from the valet. I waited by the elevators in the parking area until Jerry drove up. Silence filled the car.

Once we arrived at Adam's home, Jerry led me to a couch and left the room. My heart pounded. I sat feeling stunned. Shortly, Jerry came out of the kitchen with some hot tea and crackers.

"It was years ago," I started. "My nanny was distraught after she learned that Senator Gomez had been killed in a car accident."

Jerry sat down beside me, sipping his tea. He was quiet.

"He was quite a hero with the Latinos." I rambled. "Anyway, just after I found Hortencia crying over the newspaper, I overheard Roberto talking to one of the other creeps working for my stepfather. I can't even remember what they said, but I knew Roberto had done something. Then later when I learned about my father's death in an accident, I put two and two together. Roberto did it. I know he did. And I think there were other murders."

Jerry leaned back and pulled me into his arms. I just wanted to close my eyes and forget it all. Jerry had been in

Special Forces. Maybe he would protect me. Were Pam and Adam safe? Where were they? What was the plan? Thoughts raced through my head. I was confused, but tired. So tired. My eyelids kept trying to close. They were so heavy. Jerry said nothing but held me tight. God, why was all this happening? I couldn't think anymore.

□

TWENTY-FIVE

A DOOR SHUT in the distance and I heard voices. I opened my eyes and looked around. I was lying on Jerry's lap. I turned my head to look up at him and saw he was sound asleep, snoring softly.

Pam and Adam walked into the living room. Pam still wore the short skirt and low-cut top but had taken off the five-inch heels. She rubbed a tissue across her eyes to remove the mascara. The red wig was gone.

Adam smiled and jerked his head toward his sleeping brother. "Some protector he is," he chided.

I sat up. "What time is it?"

Jerry's arm encircled my shoulder. "What's going on guys?"

Pam wiped at her eyes with a moist tissue. "Let me get this gunk off my face and I'll meet you in the kitchen. Adam and I have some ideas."

By the time Jerry and I entered the kitchen; Adam had a pot of coffee brewing and was putting chocolate chips cookies onto a plate. My stomach grumbled. Then I realized we never ate dinner. Hope Gordon Ramsey's wouldn't be upset by a missed reservation. I reached for a cookie, bumping into Jerry when he also reached for one.

"Didn't know I was so hungry," I said.

"Yep, me too. We'll just have to try Gordon's at another date. But don't worry, I called them when we were in the café."

Pam entered the kitchen. She had traces of face cream along the edges of her face. Her long, fluffy housecoat was tied around her waist and she wore oversized slipper. "Wow, what a night!" She pulled the plate of goodies in front of her, while Adam poured her a cup of black coffee.

When we all had coffee and dessert before us, Adam sat back in his chair. He pulled a roll of 20 X 20 paper out of his back pocket and plopped it on the table in front of us.

"Now," he spread out the paper and weight it down with his coffee cup on one side and the spoon on the other. "Pam and I came up with an idea."

Jerry and I reviewed the drawing of a mangy wolf, wearing none other than Roberto's jacket. In unison, Jerry and I said "What?"

Pam leaned in. "Didn't you tell me they called Roberto, El Lobo?"

"Yes, but what has that got to do with anything?"

Before she could respond, Jerry stopped everyone. "Wait a damn minute. Tell us what happened tonight."

"Okay." Pam leaned back in her chair and took a large gulp of her hot coffee. She coughed. "Ouch. Well, I connected with Roberto."

"You're kidding," Jerry said.

"Don't get your panties all twisted. Adam was nearby in case I needed him." This time, she blew on *her* coffee before sipping. "Anyway, the wig worked. I sat next to him. I placed a few large bets and he was eating out of my hand in no time. We have a date for tomorrow night."

"Are you all crazy? What do you think you're going to do? The guy's a killer." I jumped up, staring at them all. I shivered at the thought of him being attracted to someone with long red hair. "Where is he now?"

"Sit down," Pam commanded. "He's still at the tables. Had a pile of money and didn't look like he was going anywhere soon. I promised him I'd be back tonight. Asshole was drooling by the time I was done with him."

Pam got up and went to the refrigerator. She pulled out a package of dessert rolls and placed them on a plate.

"I know this will sound crazy, but we think we have a way of handling this. The drawing is part of it." We all looked down at Adam's work.

Adam turned it around. "Of course," he began. "You'll have to do it over."

"What are you talking about? What in the world is this thing going to do?" I sat down.

Pam leaned over and touched my hand. "Remember what I said about the tattoos coming to life?" Even Jerry sighed at that one. But Pam continued. "This is our opportunity to check my theory and get rid of Roberto."

For the next ten minutes, they laid out their plans. It was just wild enough to work, but I knew I couldn't do anything that would lead to the murder of anyone. Then I figured out a way.

"Okay, but I want to make some modifications." I said.

"Like what?" Adam asked.

"I'll show you later. But first, Jerry can you run me over to my apartment?"

"Of course."

Adam took his Escalade keys from his pocket. "Jerry, take my car. No one has seen it at her place."

Jerry picked up the keys and together we headed for the garage. "We'll be back soon," I said. "I'll explain everything later."

THE SUN PEAKED over the Las Vegas Strip skyline. It took us approximately forty minutes to reach my small apartment in North Las Vegas. Jerry held my hand during the entire time.

Jerry pulled into an empty space next to my Toyota. The faded-red car still sat where we left it the previous morning. We sat in the car for a few more minutes. I told him more about how I had hidden the money and my fake IDs. Once inside the apartment, Jerry helped me pull aside the shoe rack in my closet to expose my hidden stash. Both of us worked quietly to remove documents and money from the hidden space. Jerry held up the black wig. I shook my head. We stuffed everything we had taken out and put it into a small carry-on suitcase.

Jerry looked around. "Is there anything else you want to take?"

I grabbed a few of the Robin outfits and left everything else. "No. It's time to retire both Nikki and Robin." I said.

I looked at the clothes in my arm. "But I do need something to wear."

Jerry grinned. I pulled off the blonde wig and threw it on the counter. My red hair fell in a tangle down to my shoulders. "Let's go."

As we left the apartment, Cindy, my single-mother neighbor, was heading up the stairs with a load of clean diapers. She looked at us, confused.

"Hi, Cindy." I said with a jolly voice. "How are the children doing?"

"Great." She smiled and her usual cheerfulness returned.

WHEN WE ARRIVED at Adam's house, I excused myself. I slipped into jeans and a T-shirt and pulled out my art pad. When finished with the drawing, I folded the sheet in half and went into the kitchen. "Come on, guys. We have work to do."

I spread the drawing on the table. "Now this is only a draft, but I can make it better before tonight. What I need from you is how you are going to put the tattoo together?"

Pam started. "Right. Well, I'm meeting him tonight at the same table. Oh, he'll be there. He could barely keep his hands off me. I made sure he would remember me."

Adam sighed, but said nothing.

Pam pulled a small brown, glass bottle from her bathrobe pocket. "Got some meds here that will make sure we have him under our control for several hours."
Jerry looked at the bottle. "Where in the hell did you get that?"

Both Pam and Adam laughed. "We own a tattoo parlor," Pam said, sarcastically.

Pam pointed at the drawing. "But I don't understand this drawing. I thought we wanted to turn him into a rabid wolf. Then we could call the police and wham! Problem's taken care of."

I shook my head. "And then what. There's no guarantee they will shoot him. How do we make sure he stays a wolf long enough for them to find him? And what happens if they shoot him and he turns back into a man in the morgue? How do you explain that?"
Adam looked at Pam, then back at me. "So, what's your plan? All I see is Roberto with a bald head and a messed-up body and a whole lotta tattoos. Don't forget, Jerry's tattoo stayed on him for several days."

"Just give me a few minutes and I think you will like this better. Besides, I don't think I can tattoo him if it means it gets him killed as an animal. But, if we can

arrange to get him put away for life, so
much the better."

    With that I laid a small journal on the
table.
☐

TWENTY-SIX

THE FOUR OF US stared at the small red leather book sitting in the middle of the dining room table. It was the size of a hardback novel but was held together with a blue rubber band and was stuffed with something.

Pam spoke first. "Are you going to show us what that is?"

I picked up the book and peeled off the rubber band. Slowly, I opened it and looked inside. A regular envelope slipped onto the table.

"Well?" Pam said, frowning.

"Everything." I said.

"Yes, everything. This was the proof that could put away all of them. This could put away Carlo and all his men." I shivered just thinking about it. Jerry touched my hand and several lines of concern wrinkled his forehead. "Are you alright?"

I smiled at him. "Yes. This is everything we need. I have it all."

"What do you mean?" he asked.

I took a long breath and forced myself to relax. This was it. "I have all the evidence we need."

"For your stepfather?" Adam asked.

"Yes. I have dates, names, and more important, account numbers."

Jerry opened his hand. I put the journal into it and watched as he flipped through the pages. He whistled. Then he opened the envelope and retrieved two flash drives. "What's on the flash drives?"

"I downloaded all his business information. Of course, it's two years old."

Pam rubbed her forehead and turned to Adam. "But what do we do with it?" Then Pam's eyes went wide. "The tattoos."

The rest of us stared at her.

"We've always wondered if your tattoos came to life," she said. "Now is our chance to prove it and get rid of Roberto at the same time."

I stood. "Oh. If I tattoo him with something that changes him, right? "I stopped. "But I can't do something that will kill him. I won't do that."

Adam chimed in. "What about a rabid dog? Something that will cause the police to kill him."

Jerry shook his head. "Then she would still be responsible for his death. I don't want her to be in that position. I know what it's like. She shouldn't have to live with that."

I stood. "I think I know what we can do. I'll be right back."

I went to the guest room and retrieved my tablet, drawing materials and paper. When I returned to the dining room, the three of them sat in silence. "Ready to get to work?"

"I'm game," Pam said.

Adam stood. "I'll get the tattoo supplies. We'll need them for later" He returned with a case holding a portable needle with inks and carbon paper for making the transfer.

"Yes," I said. "This should do it." I began to draw.

An hour later, Pam stood. "I better get ready while you guys pack up everything."

"I'm done," I said.

Pam came into the room and we looked at the drawing. She nodded. "Go ahead and start the transfer. And don't worry about tonight. Adam will be there to make sure nothing happens to me. Also, Pete will act as a backup."

"That should do the trick," Jerry said.

I nodded and placed the carbon transfer into a folder. While Jerry packed the equipment, I placed my gloves, goggles and apron into a bag.

Jerry picked up his phone. "I'll go pick up a van from the company and meet you at the motel. I'll put the stuff into the car. Come on, Nikki."

Pam walked into the room just as Jerry and I headed toward the front door. She wore the red wig, a black tube top, a short black skirt and her five-inch heels. She came over and put her arms around me. "We're almost done. If this works, we can start the second half of the plan."

Adam had his hair tucked under a black cap and wore all black. I almost laughed, but this was a serious situation. Adam turned around at the front door. "Let me make one call first." He hit a button on his cell. "Hey, Pete. It's Adam. Close up the shop now and meet in the parking structure of the Paris." Adam repositioned the phone to his other ear.

"Just put up a sign saying we're on vacation." Adam listened. "You're kidding."

Adam covered the phone and looked at us. "Some guy came in and wants Nikki to do a full body tattoo. He saw some of her work and doesn't want anyone else."

I looked at Adam and shook my head. "No way. Can't take the chance."

Adam returned to the phone. "Pete? Yeah, I'm back. Tell him she won't be available for a while." He paused again. "Okay. I'll call you in a couple of days. Thanks buddy." Adam hit cancel and pocketed his phone.

Pam put her hand on my shoulder. "Don't worry. When this is over, everything will get back to normal. I promise."

I shivered. "Thanks, Pam." I stepped away from her and looked at the guys. "Thank you, all of you."

With that, we walked out of the house. I didn't know what tonight held.

TWENTY-SEVEN

JERRY KEPT HIS HAND on my leg until we
reached his office. Once at the main
office, he parked his car and we piled into
an old company van. The company van had no
identity. He then drove us to a low-cost
motel on the east side of Vegas in a mostly
commercial district. He pulled behind a
room he had already reserved and together
we set up our equipment.

"I'm going to take the van across the
street," Jerry said. "I'll be right back."

"Can I go with you?" I trembled when I
watched him walk toward the door.

"You okay?" he returned and put his arm
around me. "Alright, let's hurry."

We relocated the van to the warehouse
owned by Jerry and his family. Once we hid
the van, we returned to the motel. Jerry
and I put on our latex gloves. Jerry
brought the tattooing equipment in. While
he covered the bed with a plastic tarp and
put a pile of paper towels out, I set up
the equipment and laid out the inks and my
drawing. Then we turned out the lights and
sat in the dark.

It seemed like hours, but within twenty
minutes headlights flashed across the
window. I held my breath as I listened to
voices outside. We heard a knock. I

squeezed Jerry's hand. He got up, opened the door.

"Can you help me get this piece of shit inside?" Adam asked. "For a little guy, he's heavy."

"Sure." Jerry opened the door and stepped out.

I followed him to a dark blue Ford Explorer.

"Rented?" Jerry asked.

Pam sat in the driver's seat. She opened the door and leaned out. "Some help here?"

Roberto was slumped in the passenger side, leaning against the door. Jerry walked to the car and opened the door, careful to catch the killer when he began to fall out. Jerry grabbed Roberto before he hit the ground.

"You two better put your gloves on first." Jerry said.

"Right." Pam pulled two pairs of latex gloves from her pocket and handed one to Adam. After they snapped on the gloves, Jerry picked up Roberto under his arms, while Adam lifted his feet. Together they carried him into the room and tossed him onto the plastic tarp covering the bed.

I looked down at Roberto. A small amount of blood dribbled from his nose.

Adam followed my gaze. "Sorry, I had to punch him so Pam could give him a full dose of the drug."

"Is it safe?" I asked. "How long will he be out?"

Pam, who had changed into jeans, a T-shirt and loafers, reached over and flicked him on the side of the head with her finger. "He'll be out at least four to six hours."

When I turned back to the bed, Jerry and Adam had already taken off Roberto's shirt and pants and placed him on his stomach. I stared at the leopard-print bikini underwear.

Jerry rolled the tattoo equipment toward the bed. "Guess he was expecting to have some fun. Let's get this party started."

I nodded and pulled a chair next to the half-naked man. Adam held out the tattoo needle and turned on the motor. With Roberto, I would not use sterile procedures. Who cared what kind of infections he got. My hand began to shake, but I shook off my fear. After dipping the needle into the ink, I began working on his back. In no time, my body began to react. Anger and hate coursed through me. Then, something changed and excitement filled me and I could feel my fingers tingle as I worked. Jerry, Adam and Pam stood against the opposite wall and watched me. Two hours later, I put the needle down. Pam snoozed on the small love seat, while both Jerry and Adam sat on the floor.

"Can you roll him over? I want to work on the rest of him."

Adam stood and walked over, carrying a large towel. "First let me clean off the blood and excess ink so it is not so apparent what we just did. Then we're ready to go." He wiped off Roberto and put the towels into a plastic bag he had in the corner. Together, he and Jerry looked closely at the tattoo.

"Even your ugly tattoos are beautiful," Jerry said.

I laughed and looked at my work. The tattoo on Roberto was a masterpiece of a despicable human being. It was still Roberto the man, but his hair was in patches, several teeth were missing, his eyes were bloodshot and needle marks covered the inside of his arms. Oozing meth sores could be seen on his face and upper body.

Pam came over and looked, then turned away. "He looks like a poster for a meth-using gang banger."

"Okay, turn him over, please. Since these tats will be on his arms and legs, they should be permanent."

Jerry and Adam placed another towel under Roberto and rolled him on top of it. Then Jerry pulled the little red journal out of his shirt and handed it to me. "Time to leave the real evidence."

I worked quickly and copied account numbers, dates and names over Roberto's face, arms and torso. I placed more account numbers on his legs and thighs, avoiding the briefs. Across his chest, I wrote "I killed Senator Gomez as ordered by Carlo Rinaldi." I also put down the date of the murder. On his face, I tattooed teardrops coming from both eyes to indicate how many people he had murdered. Even though I didn't know the exact number, I was sure there were more than just Senator Gomez.

Pam pulled a plastic bag from her purse and tossed a torn and bloodstained top onto the floor.

"What's that? Where did the blood come from?" I asked.

Pam pointed to her latex-gloved hand. Through the thin material, I could see a bandage wrapped around her middle finger. She held it up in defiance. "I learn from the best. Cut myself and let the blood flow. Then I just smeared it on a blouse I picked up at a thrift shop and voila. We are now ready to stage *a crime scene."*

I remembered telling her how I had spread blood on my scarf when I left it on the beach in Miami when I faked my kidnapping two years ago. Did I really go to that length to get away from Carlo? What? To get away from mansions, private schools, anything I wanted. But I knew the answer. If I hadn't left, I would be a slave to Carlo and his goons. Paying with blood. "What about DNA?" I said.

She laughed. "Honey, no one has my DNA on file. And they don't usually look for DNA unless they have a victim. Don't worry. Also, don't forget, my brother works for the FBI."

Adam cleared his throat and pulled a small plastic baggie out of his jacket pocket. "If you think that's something, wait till you see this."

Inside the baggie were several glassine envelopes filled with white powder.

"Is that what I think it is?" Jerry asked, peering closely at the bag, but not touching it.

"Sure is. And don't ask where I got it." With that, Adam opened the baggie and poured the smaller envelopes onto the bed. Five fell beside the drugged Roberto.

When done, our little group of criminals cleaned up the room. Adam ran out to the rental and came back with a cardboard box. He took out several airplane-size bottles of liquor. He sprinkled some alcohol around Roberto and pour some over his newly tattooed skin. Ouch, that will burn. Then he emptied a few of the bottles in the bathroom sink and placed them around the room. We then put all our equipment into the SUV. Jerry and Adam stripped the plastic sheeting from the bed, picked up all the blood and ink-stained towels and put them in the cardboard box he'd brought. Adam placed the now-snoring Roberto under the blankets. Roberto mumbled as we tucked him in.

"Sleep tight, jerk," I said and blew him a kiss.

Together we walked out of the room, careful to wipe down the doorknobs and any other surfaces we may have touched. Once we were back in the van Jerry, we took off our latex gloves.

"Give me all the gloves," Pam said. "I'll burn them when we get home."

We took off our gloves and handed them to Pam. She stuffed them into her pocket and got into the rental. While Jerry and I walked across the street to the warehouse, Pam and Adam moved their car across the street and parked next to Jerry's borrowed van. Each of us took out our binoculars and set ourselves up in a dark office with a clear view of the motel room. Then Jerry took out the burner cellphone, he had purchased earlier that day, and called the police.

"Hey," he breathed into the phone. "I was just driving past a motel on Fourth Street and saw a woman come running out of the last room toward the alley. She was half naked and screaming." He paused. "No, I don't know where she is. She was screaming and ran around the corner. Yeah, I think someone is still inside. The motel door is still wide open, but no one has come out."

Jerry paused. "Yeah, I'll wait here for you." He hung up and shrugged. "Another bystander who doesn't wait for the police. Oh, well."

We waited a few minutes and then he handed me another phone. "I don't think I can do it." I said.

Pam took the phone from me. "I'll do it." She said.

She took a deep breath and dialed 911. "He tried to rape me," she yelled into the phone. "I got away." Her voice broke and she made a sobbing noise. "I ran, but he's still in Room 311 at the ABC Motel on Fourth Street. Hurry." Pam punched a button on the phone to end the call and calmly turned to face us. Her eyes sparkled.

We went to the windows of one of the offices on the second floor of the building. We waited in the dark. It only took about ten minutes before a patrol car turned into the parking lot. Two policemen went first to the motel office. Jerry reached into a backpack he had taken from the van earlier and handed us two pairs of night-vision binoculars. A few minutes later, they went around to the far side of the motel, went up to the open door and looked in. They hesitated at the door and then entered. A short time later, they exited, hauling a handcuffed Roberto wearing only his leopard-print briefs. Gone was the Roberto I knew. In his place was the drawing of a meth-head, pile of shit I had tattooed on his back. I peeked down at the pile of clothing on the floor beside us and snickered.

"Glad we took his clothes. Hope the police actually get the message." I said.

"They should. You tattooed enough information on his body to write a novel." Adam said.

Together we laughed.

"Alright, you guys, time to complete Operation Carlo." Pam said.

Together the four of us left the warehouse. We tossed blood and ink-stained towels and other items into an alley dumpster as we headed back to Jerry's company. At the company, Jerry put the van back in the lot and retrieved his BMW. Pam and Adam left the rental in the company lot and picked up their Escalade, which had been left there earlier in the day.

As Jerry and I drove toward Pam and Adam's home, I felt guilty for the pleasure I felt at what I had done to Roberto. It had worked. He had turned into the very thing I had tattooed on his back. So, Pam had been right all along. Could I now do the same thing to Carlo? And what could I possibly put on him? I leaned against Jerry and slept until he kissed me on the top of the head.

"Okay, sleep. We're here."

TWENTY-EIGHT

ADAM PULLED UP TO the gate of his and Pam's new home and punched in the code. The gate swung open and he drove in. Jerry followed close behind and the gate shut behind us. Instead of parking in the garage, both cars pulled in front of the house and stopped. We opened the doors and got out. When we reached the house, the four of us moved into the foyer. Pam went into the kitchen and put on a pot of coffee. Pam poured the steaming liquid into heavy mugs and we sat around the dining room table. Jerry sat close, his hand on mine. Everyone was quiet for several minutes.

"Don't you think we should get some sleep?"

Exhausted, I yawned.

Adam shook his head. "No, we need to go ahead now. Roberto will probably contact your stepfather as soon as he returns to normal. No telling how long that will take." He took a sip from his cup and sighed. "It's already morning in New York."

"You're right." I looked at the clock on the sideboard. Three a.m. No wonder we all looked like zombies. "What do we do now?" I asked.

Jerry squeezed my hand. "I know this is uncomfortable for you. But, we're almost there. We need to finish this or you'll never be free."

I looked at Pam. Her blue eyes were bloodshot with dark circles. "I know," I stammered, "but Pam is so tired."

Pam's face brightened. She smirked. "Not that tired."

Adam stood. "Okay, let's do it."

Pam took the burner cell Jerry now held out to her and dialed Carlo's home number. She took a deep breath, closed her eyes and then shook her head.

"Hello?" she said quietly. "Hello? Is this Mr. Rinaldi?" Though she had a twinkle in her eyes, her voice sounded desperate. "I'm calling from Las Vegas. I know where Amanda is."

She stopped and listened. "No. This is not a joke. This guy Roberto kidnapped her and kept both of us as sex slaves."

She waited a few seconds. "I'm not kidding. It was a guy from New York named Roberto. Another guy, Jones, keeps us locked up and drugged if we don't follow orders. The cops nabbed Roberto last night. Jones panicked and left the house, so I got Amanda out." She paused. "Yes, I can keep her safe. She's hiding out at a friend's house." Pam paused again. "What? You want to talk to her? Okay."

Pam held out the phone.

Jerry nodded. "You can do it," he mouthed.

I took the phone. "Hello?"

"Amanda? Is that you?" Carlo said.

"Papa?" I whispered hoarsely. "Papa, I want to come home."

"What happened, Mandy? Where are you? Why did that girl talk about Roberto?"

I sobbed. God, I hated this man. "Papa," I cried into the phone. "Roberto was at the airport. He made me leave with him. Told me mama was sick. But we didn't go home. There was a van. The drive took hours. He drugged me and raped me." I sobbed. "He brought me here. I can't talk about on the phone."

I cried louder and pretended to choke. Through the moans, I gulped. "Please, Papa. Come get me." My hand shook. I handed the phone back to Pam.

"Hey, she can't talk. This has been tough on her." Pam slurred her voice. "Don't worry, Amanda's okay. We're hiding out at a motel near old Vegas." She took a deep breath. "Can you get here? I don't know how long I can keep her safe."

Pam took a deep breath. "Okay. Why don't you call me when you arrive? I'll meet you at Sam's Bar on Fremont and Tenth and take you to Amanda."

Call me on this number when you land. We can meet at the bar. But, come alone. Amanda doesn't trust anyone else." She paused again, smiled at us and hit End on the phone.

"Asshole still wanted my name," Pam put down the phone.

"Now that we're done with that, what should we tattoo on him?" Adam asked.

I looked down at my hands. They were steady. "I can do this," I said. "Let me get my drawing pad. I'll show you some ideas."

I left the room and returned with a pad and pencil. I began to draw. My hand traveled quickly over one page. I flipped to another and continued, then stopped. "I think I've got the right one."

I wadded up the first drawing and laid the second drawing on the table. Adam pulled the pad toward him and whistled. "This will work," he passed it on to Pam and Jerry.

Jerry looked at the drawing. "I like it. Shall we get started?"

Pam took the pad. "Very cool."

She pushed the drawing back and Jerry leaned in close and we studied the sketch together. The nine by twelve sheet displayed two bodies, front and back. On the back, was the sketch of an old man, rummaging through a pile of trash. He was holding a half empty bottle of booze. His hair was white, sticking out in random tufts. His mouth hung open, with two rotten teeth visible through scabbed lips. Scars covered his face, along with several warts.

However, the front of the torso was the most telling. Across his chest was a bold statement, "I am a wife abuser, murderer and gangster. The date Senator Gomez was murdered adorned an area just below his right nipple. Statements from the little red book regarding his crime adorned his arms, stomach and legs. On his forehead "I'm evil," was written in bold, block letters.

Excitement and fear coursed through me. I was ready. Now was the time for it to be over and then maybe I could save my mother. I looked at the others. "I'm going to take a shower and then let's go." With that I left the room.

TWENTY-NINE

WE SAT TOGETHER IN THE living room, dozing on chairs and sofas. It seemed like hours. The cellphone on the coffee table began to vibrate. I opened my eyes at the sound. Pam stumbled from a chair and grabbed the phone.

"Hello?" She wiped the sleep from her eyes. "Yeah, it's me."

She listened for a minute. "No, that's too public. Meet me at Sam's. Just take the strip to Fremont. Turn right. It's about two blocks up. Are you alone?"

Pam was quiet, her eyes scanned us. We held our breaths. "Okay, I'll meet you in an hour."

Pam put down the phone, looked up and smiled. "Now comes the hard part." She reached for her bag and pulled out a small brown vial. Hope there is still enough to put him under."

Adam got up from his recliner and stretched. "I'll call Sam and Pete."

I looked up in surprise. "Pete knows?"

"Of course. Why do you think he's been so cooperative in handling things while we've been traipsing around town? Both he and Sam want to help us get rid of this bozo. Sam's an old friend and Pete did all his tattoos."

Jerry got up and coughed. "Okay, let's go over the plan one more time. Nikki and I will go to the warehouse and make sure everything is set up. Pam?"

"Everyone," I interrupted. "Please call me Mandy. I'm done hiding."

"I'll meet Carlo and stall him on getting to Amanda." She looked at me. "Sam has agreed to slip him the drug."

"Pete closed the shop. He and I will be waiting in the alley out back. Once Carlo is under, we'll bring him to the warehouse." Adam said.

"What about bodyguards?" I asked.

Adam looked at me. Pete will make sure he's alone. If not, he'll let me know and we'll stop the whole thing."

"Then what?" I asked.

"Let's see how this plays out first." Adam said. "Pam will make sure he understands he won't get to see you if he doesn't come alone."

Pam stood. "I better wash my face and head out." She left the room while we went over the final details.

When Pam returned, we walked out the door together and got into our cars. Adam headed over to Sam's so Pam could meet up with Carlo. Jerry and I drove to the warehouse.

☐

THIRTY

I WAITED IN THE car while Jerry went to a large gate and removed the padlock. A sign on the fence announced future construction by Southwick Construction Company. Jerry pushed the gate open and jumped back into the car. He parked his car alongside a commercial trash container, behind some large equipment. He explained his company owned the property, which was ready for demolition. Construction of a new ten-story office building would start within a month.

We emerged from the car and went to the trunk, where Jerry took out some clothes, handed them to me and we changed.

"We're going to look like a couple of Ninjas." I took off my jeans and T-shirt and put on the all-black outfit, consisting of a sweatshirt and pants.

"Just to be safe," he handed me some black tennis shoes.

When changed, Jerry pulled out a duffle bag with the tattoo equipment and handed me two Coleman battery operated lanterns.

"We'll use these inside. But I'll use this one to get us in." He held up a five-inch tactical flashlight.

We made our way to the side of the building and located a door next to the shipping dock. Jerry pulled out a set of keys, fumbled for a few seconds and then opened the door. Metal screeched as the door brushed against the concrete floor. Together, we entered the abandoned structure. He turned on his flashlight.

"Help me lift up the loading dock door. Adam can use that when he gets here. The freight elevator is right there and he can bring Carlo up that."

We put down our equipment and together tugged on a chain to raise the heavy metal door.

"We need to go up the back stairs to the right," he said. "There was a fire in this building a few years ago and the front stairs were decimated." Jerry led me down a dark hallway. It smelled of smoke, marijuana and urine.

I tried not to breathe in the stench. "Can't we just take the elevator up?"

"Only the freight elevator still works and it's best we just leave it on the main floor for Adam. The passenger elevator fell after the fire and is just a pile of metal on the ground floor. Unfortunately, several of the elevator doors are stuck open, so stay clear of those."

"Sounds dangerous."

"Yeah, stay next to me and we'll be fine. I already scoped out a room on the fourth floor. It's the president's suite. It's large enough and has light coming in from a street lamp, so we'll need fewer lanterns."

"How can the freight elevator work if the electricity is out?" I asked.

"The freight elevator is on a backup generator. But it wouldn't matter anyway. All the lights were stolen or broken out when the building was abandoned." He handed me one of his flashlights. "Let's save the camping lights until we get to the office. However, we'll want to keep light to a minimum so we don't arouse suspicion and bring the cops."

With the flashlight in one hand and the duffle bag over his shoulder, Jerry held my hand and led me through the dark building and up the back stairs. A few times, I stumbled over refuse, but Jerry caught me and held on until we finally arrived on the fourth floor.

"You can turn on your flashlight. But, just stay to the right of the hallway," Jerry said, his flashlight creating ghostly shapes as he lit the passage in front of us. "The open elevator door is about halfway down on the left."

"This way." He pointed the flashlight down the dreary hallway. Halfway down the corridor, a dark mass could be seen across from the fourth door on the right. I stopped and took a small step forward. My flashlight was dim, but I used it to read each door we passed. Dark frosted windows stared back. We passed Human Resources and Sales when I stumbled over a mat on the floor and stepped back. Jerry shined his light on the door behind me. "M—k—t—g" was all that was left of the title on the door.

"Be careful," Jerry cautioned. He reached out and pulled me back.

"Is that the elevator?"

He shined his light into the open shaft. "Yep. The doors are stuck open. We need to put up caution tape, but it hasn't happened yet. So just be careful. Stay close."

We continued to move along the hall, passing a door marked "Vice President" to a wood-paneled door. He pushed the door open and ushered me in. The outer office was void of furniture. We walked through to an office with large paned windows, mostly painted gray. A street lamp illuminated the room with a faint glow. A large executive desk, a credenza and several folding chairs were crowded into the center of the inner office. Jerry took the lanterns from me and placed one just under the desk and turned it on. More light filled the room. He turned off his flashlight.

Together, we placed the credenza closer
to the desk and put one chair in front of
it. I sat down but found it uncomfortable.
Jerry took the flashlight and left for a
few minutes. I heard a strange noise and
turned. A light hit the office door and a
minute later Jerry entered, rolling in a
stool on wheels. He turned off the
flashlight.

For the next several minutes, we worked
on setting up the portable gear. We placed
a plastic sheet on the desk, then shut off
the lantern. With only the ambient light
from outside, we sat stretched out on a
blanket Jerry had brought from his car and
used the duffle bag as a pillow.

Silence filled the darkness.□

THIRTY-ONE

THE CONSTANT IN AND out of our breaths punctuated the silence. We reclined on the floor with our heads on the duffle bag and waited.

"Can you do this?" Jerry asked after a while.

"Yes, I think so."

He took my hand and placed it on his chest. His heart beat a steady thump in his chest. "I'll be with you the entire time."

I heard a siren in the distance.

Jerry squeezed my hand. "What will you do when this is over? Go back to New York? To your mom?"

I took a deep breath. "I don't know. I never thought this day would come. I'm not sure I even want to go home." I rolled toward Jerry.

He moved over and kissed my forehead. "Whatever you decide, I'll support you."

A door banged in the distance and a few minutes later I could hear the grinding of the freight elevator struggling up the shaft.

"They're here." Jerry got up and went to the door.

"Does Adam know where to go?" I asked.

"He knows we are on the fourth floor. I'll go down to the elevator and meet him. You okay to stay here alone?"

"I think so."

"Be right back." He turned on his flashlight and went down the hall, leaving the door open.

While he was gone, I looked at my hands. They trembled. My insides churned. Acid climbed up my throat. I gagged.

The door opened and Adam, Jerry and Pete came into the room carrying Carlo. Pam followed closely behind.

"Fat son-of-a-bitch," Adam groaned, placing Carlo's overweight body on the desk. I looked at my stepfather and moved back.

Adam unbuttoned Carlo's shirt. "Pete, you better leave. You've done enough."

Pete came over and gave me a hug. "I'm rooting for you, Mandy. Can I call you Mandy now?"

"Sure," I said and hugged him back.

Pete nodded to everyone and left. A few minutes later, we heard him drive away.

Jerry turned and looked at me. He came over. "You don't have to do this," he said. I took a deep breath. "Yes. I do." I pulled myself together and approached the now half-naked man on the table.

"Put him on his back," I said. "Let me tattoo his front first."

Pam pulled a small case from her purse and came forward with a syringe to inject more sedative into Carlo. "This will keep him for a few more hours," she said. Her hand began to shake and she dropped the syringe, glass breaking on impact.

I looked up at Pam. Beads of sweat trickled down the side of her face. "Pam, are you okay?"

She nodded, but grimaced.

"Adam," I pointed at Pam. "I think something's wrong."

Adam rushed to her and took her hands as she crumpled to the floor and began to heave. Adam sniffled and a tear ran down his face. "We didn't tell you before, but Pam's pregnant."

Jerry strode toward Pam. "Pregnant? She shouldn't even be here. What were you thinking after she lost the last baby?"

"I'm okay," Pam insisted. She began to heave again. "It's probably just late morning sickness."

I dropped the tattoo needle and looked at the dark windows. It was still night. I went to Pam and touched her forehead. "Morning sickness my ass. She's burning up."

Adam had dropped to his knees and was now cradling Pam, who tried to push him away.

"I'm fine." she insisted and tried to rise.

"Pam," I called. "You can't."

She again tried to get up but fell back to the floor.

Jerry shook his head and looked at Carlo. "No. We should shut this down. We can't jeopardize Pam's health just to get this scumbag."

"No," Pam stared at Carlo and whispered. "If we don't do this, Carlo will just come after Amanda and have her killed. He knows she's here. If he doesn't kill her it could be worse." Pam coughed. Her face turned white.

"Fine." Jerry said. "But you need to get out of here and to the ER." He pointed down at the still-sleeping Carlo. "We'll take care of him."

Adam pulled Pam to her feet. "I agree."
Jerry picked up his flashlight. "I'll light the way. Come on, let's get her to the car."

Jerry lifted Pam into Adam's arms. Pam complained, then gagged.

Jerry turned to me. "I'll be right back."

A short while later, I heard Adam's car drive away. When Jerry returned, he helped me prepare Carlo. We pulled his shirt the rest of the way off. Carlo continued to snore loudly. Foregoing any lubricant, I took a razor and began to shave the thick patch of hair from his back. The Bic shaver grated against his dry skin. I removed the last of the hair.

"I think I'll do the big tattoo first." I said. "Can you help me turn him onto his back?"

Jerry stepped forward and together we turned over the sleeping man. This hair on his chest was even thicker. I ran the razor over his back and removed most of the hair. Then, with a small sterile pad, I applied a thin layer of Vaseline. I took out the tattoo transfer from the duffle bag and placed it on Carlo's skin. I started to press on the carbon paper to set the transfer when a door slammed downstairs.

"That can't be Adam," Jerry said. "I'll go check. Be right back." He picked up the lantern and pulled out a small handgun from a holster under his shirt.

"I didn't know you brought a gun." I said.

"Just in case," he said. "Wait here."

"Don't worry about me. I'll be fine." I rubbed the paper on Carlo's skin to allow the carbon ink to transfer to set when a loud bang echoed in the building. I jumped and dropped the transfer. It sounded like a gunshot.

"Mandy. Run." Jerry screamed from somewhere below.
□

THIRTY-TWO

"JERRY?" I JUMPED UP and stepped forward. Something pulled me back. I fell against the desk.

"Mandy, what the hell?" Carlo said.

I turned and saw Carlo's eyes wide open. He sat on the edge of the desk, dressed only in his pants. I tried to move away, but he held onto my shirt.

"Let me go," I screamed and yelled Jerry's name.

"Where are you going? What's going on?" Carlo's speech slurred, but he held tight. He grabbed my upper arm and pulled me closer. "You're safe now. Daddy's here."

I tried to pull away. "Let me go."

Carlo tugged me into an embrace. The stubble on his chest scraped against my face. I struggled, but he had my arms pinned by my side. He moved one hand up and started stroking my hair. I tried to push him away, but he stood and put his face into my neck, taking a deep breath.

"I see you still wear that perfume," he whispered into my ear.

I tried to push him away. I opened my mouth to scream when his face moved in front of me and his mouth came down on mine. Before I could react, his tongue found its way into my mouth. I choked and jerked my head back. He grabbed the back of my head and held me tight as he forced himself on me. He moved back, his saliva dripping from my face. Carlo began pulling at my clothes. I could not break free from his grip.

"Let me go," I yelled. He ignored me and tore at my sweatshirt. His hand came up under my top. His breath came in short bursts as he rubbed against me. He moved down to my pants and began pulling them down. I could feel the elastic cutting into my waist. He put his lips on mine once again. I held my teeth together.

Bile rose from my stomach and burned my throat. I swallowed hard. Could it really be true the man who raised me now tried to rape me? I let my body go limp and began to fall to the floor. Surprised, he loosened his grip.

I fell to the floor and reached for the lantern. I grabbed it by the handle. Carlo pulled at me and I twisted away and swung. The lantern connected to the side of his head and the glass shattered. Batteries fell out and rolled across the floor, leaving us both in darkness.

Carlo screamed in pain and crumpled to the floor "Mandy, what are you doing? I'm here to save you."

I backed away, getting closer to the door. I screamed at Carlo. "You, you're a killer. You killed my father. Did you think I would never figure it out?"

Carlo moaned in pain, holding his bloody head. "You bitch. You're just like your mother."

He took a deep breath and moved forward, reaching for me. The only illumination in the room came the outside streetlight. I shoved him away and crawled to the door. I stood and pulled open the door and went into the vestibule. I raced to the outer door and pulled it open and entered the darkness.

Carlo yelled behind me. "Come back here. You mean everything to me. What did they do to you?"

I remembered Jerry's words when we came in, "Keep to the right." Leaving the office, I turned and clung to the left wall. Slowly, I made my way to the next doorway. I remembered the open elevator shaft, which was on the left side when we came in, but now that I was going in the opposite direction, I stayed to the left.
Jerry! Where was Jerry?

The door opened behind me.

"Mandy, I love you." Carlo's pained voice said. "I forgive you."

I flattened myself into a doorway and remained quiet.

"I love you," Carlo called out.

I heard him stumble in the darkness as he moved closer. I needed to move.

I bit my tongue and held my breath. In the dark, I could hear Carlo feeling his way along the hall. I waited.

"Mandy?" he yelled into the darkness. "Where are you? I forgive you for leaving me. Please, Mandy."

I came to another door and reached for the knob. Locked. I felt the pane above the knob and could feel the peeling letter "M". I started to move out of the doorway, but a faint movement caught my attention.

"Mandy, we'll start over. Your mother's nothing but a drunk anyway. Been at a rehab center for months now." Carlo bumped an empty can and it clattered down the hall.

"Shit! Mandy? Where are you? I can't see a damn thing." I could smell the tobacco on his breath.

I remembered my mother's bruised face. My blood boiled. I hated this man. He was so close, I could smell his sweat. I peeked out of the doorway and saw a pale blur in the darkness. I reached out my left arm and began to move along the hallway.

"Mandy?" Carlo called, from a few feet away. "I don't care about the money or the diamonds. You were the one who took them, weren't you?"

He breathed out and the odor of garlic, whisky and tobacco filled the hall. How did he get so close?

"Wherever you have them is fine."

Afraid to make noise, I stopped, my back against the recessed door. Thank God for my black clothing. I moved again, my foot crunched on a piece of glass. Carlo reached through the darkness and grabbed me. I screamed and pushed him.

"Got ya," he laughed before he threw me on the floor. I fell against the wall and *Carlo pulled me into the hall and straddled me.* I screamed. He grabbed my wrists and twisted them over my head. With his other hand, he slipped his hand under my sweatshirt.

"Oh, Mandy. You have no idea how long I have wanted you and now you are mine."

He tore at my pants. His breath came in short gasps as he took his one hand off me and began to pull at his zipper. He lifted himself up to undo his belt. I jerked free and pushed him back. He fell into a sitting position and laughed. In the faint light from a window down the hall, I saw him stand and remove his belt.

My chest became hot and began to burn. I rolled onto my side and my locket fell out of the sweatshirt and touched the floor. A bright light grew until I was blinded. I glared at Carlo. He stood with his belt in his hands with a look of shock on his face.

"You. It can't be," he screamed. "No!"

Carlo stumbled back across the hall and tripped over his falling pants. He disappeared into the darkness. His scream echoed up the elevator shaft, followed by a thud.

I screamed and struggled to a sitting position.

"You're safe now." A soft voice whispered. I turned my head, but the light was too bright.

"Daddy?" I whispered. The light faded, and I was left sitting in the dark.

◻

THIRTY-THREE

I WATCHED A FAINT glow brighten the painted-over window at the end of the long hallway. One small sliver of light peeked through a hole in the silver paint and landed a few inches from where I sat. I got on my knees and prayed.

Thank you, Lord. For giving me back my life.

*Footsteps sounde*d on the stairs and a beam of a light bobbed up and down *in the stairwell.* The beam reached the landing and traveled toward me. A tall man stood and pointed his flashlight at me. I froze.

"Mandy? Are you okay?" Jerry rushed forward then dropped down and took me in his arms.

"Yes," I moaned. "But I killed him."

"What? How?" Jerry held me close.

"He tried to rape me," Hot tears streamed down my face. "I kicked him. He tripped over his pants and he fell down the shaft."

Jerry looked at the opening behind him, now visible in the morning light. "Mandy, you couldn't have kicked him that far. You didn't kill him. It was an accident. Either way, it's over." He stood and pulled me to my feet.

Then I *no*ticed blood on Jerry's nose. "You're hurt."

Behind Jerry another light bobbed up the stairs. I grabbed Jerry. "Someone's coming."

Jerry turned and watched a large figure approach. Jerry turned his flashlight toward the stairs. I stepped behind Jerry as Max came into view.

"Oh, my God," I gasped. "It's Max."

Max continued to move forward. I pulled on Jerry. Max stopped a few feet away.

"Hello, Mandy."

I peered around Jerry. Why didn't Jerry take out his gun? Why were we standing here? I clung to Jerry.

"Where's Carlo?" Max asked, looking around.

I closed my eyes and waited for a loud bang. Jerry moved toward Max.

"He's down the shaft. He tried to rape her."

Max stepped over and shined his light down the opening onto Carlo's broken and twisted body. "He's dead."

I stared at the two men. What the hell? Max held out his hand to Jerry. Jerry actually took it! What was going on? Confused, I stared at both of the men.

"Sorry I hit you back there. Had no idea who you were." Jerry said.

"Miss Mandy, I'm sorry I couldn't help you sooner. You did a good job of hiding."

Confused, I stood rooted to the spot. "I don't understand?"

"I've always been helping you," he said. "It's the least I could do for your father. He was my best friend."

"My father?" I sat down on the bottom stair. "What are you talking about?"

"The only reason I took the job with Carlo was to watch out for you and your mother. Not only was I a good friend of your father's, but I work with the FBI."

FBI? I was really getting confused.

"Once we found out you were still alive, I promised your mother I would make sure you made it home safe." Max moved closer and put his hand on my shoulder. "I'm sorry I couldn't tell you. I was undercover and you were just a kid when I started working for Carlo. Your mother and I felt we just couldn't take the chance."

"Carlo killed my father," I said to
Max.

"Yes, I know. Now you and your man need
to get out of here. I'll take care of
Carlo."

Jerry took my hand and waved his
flashlight toward the office we had used.
"We need to clean up things. There's tattoo
equipment in the room a few doors down."

When the band of light passed across
Max, I noticed fresh blood on his shoulder.

"You're bleeding," I said.

Max touched his shoulder and winced.
"Through and through." He took a small
handgun from his pocket and handed it to
Jerry.

"Sorry, man. I didn't know." Jerry took
the gun and stuck it in his waistband.

"How could you? You were just trying to
protect Miss Mandy." Max took out a
handkerchief and slipped it under his
jacket. "Now, just tell me how to access
the elevator shaft and I'll take care of
everything. You can come back in a couple
of days and get your equipment. Everything
will be taken care of by then. The two of
you scram."

Jerry and I walked out of the building.

As Jerry helped me into the car, I stopped.

"Jerry, something happened in there."
"I know. But, it's over now."

"No. You don't understand. My locket got really hot and a light came out." I hung my head. "I know it sounds crazy."

"Where is your locket?"

I reached under my shirt and found it tucked safely between my breasts. I pulled it out, slipped it over my neck and handed it to him.

"It looks fine." He opened the locket and took out the small folded piece of paper. I took it and unfolded it on my lap. It was blank. I looked at Jerry.

"Could it have been?" I shook my head.

"God works in miraculous ways," he said. "Let's get out of here and go check on Pam. You call Adam and I'll get us to the hospital."

The morning was already threatening to be a scorcher as we drove away.
☐

THIRTY-FOUR

KATHRYNE'S HANDS SHOOK when she placed the veil on my head. She tried to be careful not to mess up my hair. I reached up and took her hand.

"Relax, mom." I held her hands in mine.

My mother laughed, bent down and kissed me on the cheek. "I don't want to smudge your make up."

"Mom, I'm so glad you're doing well. And I'm sorry for making you think I was dead. I just didn't know any other way to get away from Carlo and I was so mad."

"Mandy, we don't have to think about Carlo anymore. Max took care of everything."

"Yes. Kind of prophetic. Carlo killed dad in a car accident and Max makes it look like Carlo died in a car accident. Can't say I'm sorry. But I was surprised about Max."

The corners of Kathryne's lips rose slightly. "Max approached me when you were little and told me about being friends with your father. I didn't find out about his FBI connections until you disappeared. That's when Max and I set it up for Carlo to think I was an alcoholic. Max had an easy time convincing him to put me in a rehab center. I thought about getting out of the marriage years ago, but knew he would never let me go, and I had no proof of what he had done."

She put another tiny flower in my hair. "I made sure Max was always with you. You were never really in danger." She looked in the mirror and adjusted her hair. "You surprised us all when you stole all that money. Smart of you to replace the diamonds with pebbles. He didn't even know they were gone for months. You should have heard him scream when he discovered the loss. Threatened to kill all his men."

We both laughed.

"Max told me the FBI was embarrassed when you outsmarted them. They lost your after Miami and began to think you were dead. That's why Max could stage the car accident for Carlo's body. Can you imagine how it would look that the FBI lost you two years ago and was unable to locate you?"

"Will I get in trouble?"

"No. Max convinced them you had no other option. So, any charges have been dropped. Not that I care," she added. "But what did you do with the diamonds? Can't imagine you found anyone to buy them."

"Never wanted the diamonds. Just wanted him to suffer, so I threw them in the Mississippi."

Kathryne chuckled. "Where they belong. I don't think we should ever tell anyone there are over two million dollars of diamonds in the Mississippi mud."

There was a knock on the door. My mother opened the door to Pam. Hortencia stood behind her.

"You ready?" Pam asked. She wore a lavender cocktail dress and held a bouquet of lavender roses. She turned to me. "Time for us to walk in."

Kathryne checked her makeup. She kissed me one more time. "I love you, Amanda."

I went out the door with Pam and Hortencia.

Hortencia hastened down the aisle to her seat in the front row and sat next to Jorge. Jorge had been cleared of all corruption and racketeering charges after testifying against Carlo and several other New York mobsters involved in Carlo's dealings. Even the Albany Mayor had been indicted. The book I turned over to the FBI also cemented Jorge's innocence and he was finally able to connect with the love of his life.

Pam led the way up the aisle. I followed behind.

As Pam stepped up on the dais, she looked back at Pete and his wife sitting in

the first row. Alicia, Pete's wife, looked
ready to pop out her little girl any
minute. I wondered how Pete was going to
fit those tattoos on his already covered
body. The new owner of Las Vegas Tattoo,
Pete sat tall and proud. I passed Jerry's
and Adam's parents sitting side by side.
They smiled at me and his mother squeezed
her husband's hand. Mr. Southwick decided
to retire within a year and leave the
construction company to his two sons. It
was time for he and his wife to travel the
world and let others take over.

I stepped up on the stage and looked at
three favorite men. Jerry, my loving
husband and soon-to-be father of our child
winked at me. Adam, new CFO of Southwick
Construction, had decided to go straight
and run a real business, of course, with
Pam's genius computer and financial skills.
And, Max, my stepfather to be, stood
straight and towered over the other two.
Beads of sweat glistened on his bald, black
head. When he saw me looking at him, his
mouth widened in a smile. The gold tooth
had been replaced with a white cap and his
teeth lit up his dark face.

Ave Maria began to play. Pete's now
five-year-old son held two-year-old Nicole
Pamela Southwick's hand as they brought the
rings on a velvet pillow and came to the
front. The doors opened. My mother stepped
through and slowly moved toward us. She
raised her eyes and looked up at her groom.
Both smiled.

As she moved closer, I whispered to Max. "If I haven't said it before, thank you. Thank you for taking care of me. Thank you for taking care of my mom. And, I know you'll make a great president of Bartoli Enterprises."

Max bowed his head slightly and I could have sworn there were tears in his eyes. "Anything for my two favorite ladies."

A sweet voice lifted into the rafters. I stood looking at my brand new, equal opportunity family and I felt blessed and happy.

THE END